A Fleeting Glimpse

Stories about Choices

by K. E. Swope

Leaning Rock Press

Copyright © 2024, Kathleen E. Swope

All rights reserved. No parts of this publication may be reproduced, stored in a database or retrieval system, or transmitted, in any form or by any means, without the prior permission of the author or publisher except by a reviewer who may quote brief passages in a review.

Leaning Rock Press
Gales Ferry, CT 06335
leaningrockpress@gmail.com
www.leaningrockpress.com

978-1-960596-30-7, Hardcover
978-1-960596-31-4, Softcover

Library of Congress Control Number: 2024908021

Publisher's Cataloging-in-Publication Data
(Prepared by Cassidy Cataloguing's PCIP Service)

Names:	Swope, K. E., author.
Title:	A fleeting glimpse : stories about choices / by K.E. Swope.
Description:	Gales Ferry, CT : Leaning Rock Press, [2024]
	Identifiers: ISBN: 978-1-960596-30-7 (hardcover) | 978-1-960596-31-4 (softcover) | LCCN: 2024908021
Subjects:	LCSH: Choice (Psychology)--Fiction. | Automobile racing drivers--Fiction. | Political campaigns--Fiction. | Bottles--Social aspects--Fiction. | Bank robberies--Fiction. | LCGFT: Short stories. | BISAC: FICTION / Short Stories.
Classification:	LCC: PS3619.W662 F54 2024 | DDC: 813/.6--dc23

Printed in the United States of America

This book is dedicated to the talented writers
I've met in so many writing groups over the years.
Without your encouragement,
I would never have completed these stories.

Table of Contents

FOREWORD 1
Vote For Judy 3
Dog Daze. 9
Knitting Circle with Gun. 21
Leaf Battle 29
Neighborly. 35
Natural Talent. 41
Happily Ever After 51
The Day the Sky Fell 59
Amos and the Deaconess 71
Office Etiquette. 79
Promise Made, Promise Kept 89
My First Body 99
Betrayal 113
Disputed Remains 121
Funeral Junkie. 129
Redemption. 135
Good Day, Bad Day 147
The Bare Essentials. 161
Going Home 169
Man to Man. 175
Breakdown 183
Acknowledgments 197
About the Author. 198

FOREWORD

When I decided to try my hand at creative writing, I was coming from an environment of technical writing that had to be precise and concise. It's been fun learning a whole new way of presenting ideas to readers.

During these 30 years of learning, I have sat through classes on creative writing and participated in numerous writing groups. Along the way, I've met wonderful people who were also interested in expanding their ability to express themselves in new ways.

I've discovered that I like writing short fiction, which is a logical extension of the concise writing of my work experience. Each of these stories provides a small glimpse into someone's life, when a choice had to be made. When I saw that, I asked myself "Why did that happen?" or "What happened next?" For example, my favorite story in this collection, "Vote for Judy," arose out of noticing such a sign as I passed it along the side of the road. Another favorite, "Bare Essentials," developed from hearing about such a cruise and wondering what would happen if someone was placed in such a situation, unknowingly. I wrote "Promise Made, Promise Kept" because my husband's fascination with auto racing made me say one day, "I wonder what it's like to drive a race car." So he sent me to a one-day driving class for races—and he went, too.

Everyone has stories to tell. What are yours?

K. E. Swope

Vote For Judy

I first noticed him several weeks before the election, late afternoon of a gray New England day. It was the same date I had lost my Paul at age nine, five years earlier.

Luckily for other drivers, I was stopped at a red light. Otherwise, I would have been oblivious to my surroundings and caused an accident. Five years seems like a long time, but to me it was yesterday. My heart began aching all over again, a feeling I thought I had long buried.

When this boy turned, I saw only his size was similar. There he stood, all four feet of him, the hood of a yellow rain slicker around his neck and water droplets on his brown curls. With both hands he grasped a broomstick supporting a cardboard sign. Crooked orange letters spelled out "Vote for Judy." A dribble of excess paint extended the "y" to the bottom edge.

Although I drove home from work the same way every day, I had not seen him before. Maybe it was his first day on that corner, a good location with cars stopped at the traffic light.

Reflexes took over. I smiled and waved. He caught the movement and smiled back. Then he jiggled his sign up and down, pointed to the words, and shouted something I couldn't hear. Just then the car behind me began honking because the light had turned green, so I had to move on.

In my dreams that night I saw again the image of red stuck in half-melted ice. It was the back of Paul's jacket. Although I ran and ran, I could never reach him.

Waking in a cold sweat, I tried to count backward from one hundred, a calming mechanism that usually relaxed me enough to go back to sleep. By the time I reached fifteen, I realized it wasn't working, so I got up and made a pot of tea. With a steaming cup of oolong sitting before me and pen in hand, I wrote in my journal about the encounter.

Then I got an inspiration—perhaps I could turn the shock into something positive, something I could do to help this other Paul.

The next morning when I took the mail to my boss at the radio station, I mentioned the boy and my idea. Ross grunted into his newspaper and reached over to queue up the next blues song. He didn't like new ideas from anyone else.

On my way home, I looked for the boy again. I almost missed him among the rushing adults. Then he appeared, camouflaged by a gray hooded sweatshirt, like the one my son had worn in warm weather. Before I could catch his attention, the driver in the car behind me blew three sharp blasts and I had to move.

The next day, Wednesday, I worked late, typing press releases for a new talk program to boost advertising income. As the only paid employee, I got all the extra tasks Ross didn't have time to do. So it was dark by the time I passed Paul's corner. The boy wasn't there.

On Thursday and Friday, Paul was there again, a small boy with a message ignored by most people passing by, both in cars and on foot. Both days I waved, uncertain whether he saw me. I thought his mother must be proud of him, as I had been of Paul.

That weekend I was drawn to Paul's corner. I looked for him both days, but he wasn't there. Somehow, I felt empty inside, hoping nothing had happened to him.

On Monday, Ross looked up when I delivered the mail. "Y'know, Di, I was thinkin' about that idea you had," he said, sipping his coffee from a mug with the station logo. "That little boy campaignin' for his mom. Great human interest stuff. Could boost our ratings."

He flipped the switch to start the second CD player. Joe Henderson's saxophone began playing in the studio and on people's radios.

"So, you want the assignment, or what?"

"Me?"

Ross set his mug down on a lopsided pile of papers but grabbed it before the contents spilled. "Sure. You been workin' here, what, two, three years? Answerin' phones, typin' letters, and all. Here's your chance if you want it."

A Fleeting Glimpse

"Do I! Thanks." I started out the door.

"Wait," Ross called out. "On your own time. Work 'round here still needs doin'. But do a decent job, and, well, we'll see."

"Sure."

Closing the door behind me, I heard Ross open up the microphone. "That was Joe Henderson on WCTX. This is Doctor Jazz. The doctor is in! Call me at...."

For the rest of the day I had trouble concentrating while I typed letters and answered phones. I read the guidelines for interview etiquette Ross gave volunteers who showed up to try news reporting. Many wanted to be the next Walter Cronkite and figured an easy beginning was to volunteer at the local radio station. Most left after a month or two, but another one usually showed up before long.

After three years of barely covering my bills, I was eager to try something more challenging and profitable. Even waiting tables on weekends wouldn't cover extras, like car repairs. What I probably needed was another car, unthinkable without extra money.

I left promptly at five o'clock, to face gray skies, although the morning had been cloudless. If I was lucky, the rain would hold off until after I talked to Paul.

I wasn't lucky. As I pulled up to the stop sign, the skies opened. There he stood in the downpour, his sign held aloft and the hood on his yellow slicker pulled as far forward as possible. His head tilted forward and his shoulders drooped, but the painted message defied the rain—"Vote for Judy."

In the dampness, my car stalled. Paul looked up at the laboring attempts of my starter. I thought I saw him smile just as the engine started. I had to move before I lost power altogether in the dampness.

At home I began to write up a few notes. This was going to be a great story—maybe I could finally dump my clunker of a car.

On Tuesday afternoon, extra work for Ross delayed me until after five o'clock. I was surprised to find the boy still on his corner.

At the corner, Paul returned my wave. I parked nearby and headed for my big break. As I approached, I held out an unopened can of soda. "Want a drink? That looks like thirsty work."

"No, thanks, but it was nice of you to offer. Are you a registered voter in the second district?"

"Why, no, I live in the sixth district."

"Oh." He looked past me for more likely targets.

"But I work at a radio station," I offered, walking closer to hand him a business card. "WCTX? Maybe you've heard of it? We broadcast jazz all the time."

He took the card, shaking his head. "Nope, my mom just listens to the news station."

"We do advertise for political candidates, though."

"But that costs money, doesn't it?"

"Not if it's a special story about a youngster taking an interest in politics."

By the wrinkle in his forehead, I knew I had him thinking.

"How about if we talk about it." I looked around. "Is there a place to sit? Or can I come to your house and talk with your family?"

I thought I saw panic in his eyes for a moment. His eyes locked on mine. "Must you?"

"Sit down? Well, it would be easier for me to take notes. Besides I feel like a tower looming over you."

His laughter sounded so much like my Paul's. "I meant, must you talk to my mom? She doesn't get home until after six, and she's always tired."

"I guess you can give me enough information. But I would like to sit down."

We settled ourselves on a low concrete wall around one of the maple trees lining the street. While he braced the sign so that passing motorists could still read his message, I studied this boy who reminded me so much of my own.

His brown curls in back flipped up just above his shirt, leaving a few ends trapped beneath the faded blue collar. On the shirt a dark yellow blob looked like mustard, and the top button was hanging by only a few strands of thread. The cuffs of his jeans had brown splotches, probably dried mud. I pulled my attention back to the interview.

"Okay, let's start. What's your name?"

"My name is Christopher Caulkins and I'm ten years old." He flashed a smile, exposing a gap between his front teeth. "Mom calls me Christopher Caboose because I have two brothers in college."

"Well, Christopher, it's great that you're getting involved in our elective process. Did you make the sign yourself?"

"Yep, I found an old broom and a half-used can of paint in the cellar. My dad used to do a lot of work around the house. I can always find neat stuff down there."

"What's your dad's name?"

Christopher shrugged. "Is it important?"

"Isn't it important to you?"

"Mom says it shouldn't be since he left us."

I cleared my throat. "So, tell me why you spend your afternoons here?"

He sat up straight. "It's the responsibility of every voter to fulfill their civic duty and vote for good officials. Otherwise, they shouldn't complain when things don't go the way they want."

"I see." I wrote down his words. "You seem to know a lot about it."

"For my age, you mean." His voice was not angry, just tired. "I should. Mom's been our representative ever since I remember. She's very good at what she does, don't you know?" He looked at me, questioning with his eyes.

"Actually, I don't, since I live in another voting district. I'm not familiar with officials in other areas. Now, let me see, what...?"

The blast of the factory steam whistle interrupted me. Christopher jumped up

"Omigosh, it's six o'clock. I'm late!" He grabbed his sign and raced away without a backward glance.

I spent several hours that evening writing and revising my story. It should help Christopher's mother win reelection.

Ross was on the air when I took in the mail the next morning. While I waited at my desk to show him my story, I read it again. Ross was going to love this, and so would our listeners, especially the mothers. Maybe it would get picked up by one of the wire services and gain national recognition. It could make my career in radio journalism.

The phone interrupted my daydream. Work took precedence.

"Good morning. WCTX--your choice for cool jazz, hot topics, and what's happening in Millville. May I help you?"

"Good morning," replied a firm female voice. "This is representative Caulkins from the second district. I found a business card from your station in my son's jeans this morning. However, no name was on it. What has my son been doing?"

I cleared my throat. "Diane Evans speaking, Mrs. Caulkins. I saw Christopher campaigning on the street corner and want to do a story about it. I'm glad you called because I need your permission."

A pause. "Oh, he was campaigning? And when was that?"

"I've seen him there since last week. You didn't know?"

I heard a deep sigh. "I had no idea, although I'm relieved it was something constructive. It's hard being a single parent, Mrs., Miss…?"

"It's Mrs.," I replied, my voice cracking. I remembered how impossible it was to keep track of an active nine-year-old boy.

"Then you can probably understand how worrisome it is to work full time when you have children."

"Yes." I kept my voice even. I remembered broken ice with the red knit cap bobbing in the open water.

The woman's voice on the other end continued, "It can be a great blessing…and a great responsibility." She sighed. "I'll need to see a copy of anything you plan to air."

"Of course. For accuracy, would you spell your name for me? I live in a different district and…."

"No need to apologize. It's Sherry, like the wine, S-H-E-R-R-Y, Caulkins, C-A-U-L-K-I-N-S. Do you have that?"

I couldn't answer. I stopped writing and stared at the paper. I began, "But…" and stopped.

"Mrs. Evans, are you there?"

"Ah, yes, Mrs. Caulkins, did you say Sherry? I thought it was Judy."

A short pause, then a light laugh. "You really are from across town. No, I'm Sherry. Judy D'Amico is my opponent, and to tell you the truth, she's giving me the biggest challenge of the four campaigns I've been through."

After she hung up, I sat and stared at the crinkled paper in my hand.

Dog Daze

For her husband's funeral, Phoebe Hardy wore black, the proper thing to do. She kept her eyes downcast and mumbled her thanks to people's remembrances of David. Their pastor and two church members expressed sadness that he hadn't been around to celebrate his upcoming fortieth wedding anniversary. Sometimes Phoebe dabbed at her eyes with a lace handkerchief, but she never shed a tear. She held her feelings deep, away from critical eyes.

David's brother and sister, with their spouses, flew in for a week. Phoebe had invited them to stay with her. It was the proper thing to do. They brought Aunt Sophie, the elderly aunt who had raised the three siblings after their parents died. The four expected guests tried to be helpful, but Aunt Sophie demanded vegetarian meals and clean towels every day. Phoebe bought a vegetarian cookbook and, knowing her duty, washed linens every morning.

After the funeral, Aunt Sophie offered to stay longer while Phoebe became accustomed to life alone. Phoebe panicked, foreseeing a new tyrant in her house. She stammered her thanks while she tried to think of a way to decline without seeming rude. Silently she said a prayer of thanks when David's brother pointed out that their airline tickets allowed no refunds. They would lose hundreds of dollars by changing their reservations for later. Money had always been important to David and his family, for which Phoebe was now grateful.

Finally, David's relatives left. Aunt Sophie wept openly, with her arms clasped tightly around Phoebe. For the hundredth time, Phoebe heard that David as the youngest had always been his aunt's favorite.

That Sophie felt so close to him in this house, surrounded by his things. Phoebe feared Sophie would stay on, despite paying extra on her airline flight. Luckily, the family's Midwestern frugality took her away in a taxi with the others.

Phoebe closed the front door behind them and turned the lock. She looked around. Sophie was right—she was surrounded by David's things. She had to do something about that eventually. For the rest of this day she would indulge herself.

She headed for the den, the room David had called the library. His presence still permeated the room. The seat cushion on his high-backed, overstuffed chair had been sculpted by his body and its leather held the cherry scent of his favorite pipe tobacco. The maple desk in the corner had been his domain, less intimidating now that his brother had helped Phoebe decipher the bills and receipts. Perhaps he would want David's leather chair. She should have asked, but she could take care of that later.

For now she gloated over all the lovely books. Such a feast spread before her. Many of them she had wanted to read but David had too many demands on her time. Which book should she choose as an appetizer?

The telephone on the desk rang before she could make a choice. She considered not answering it but discarded that notion. If she didn't answer, the concerned well wisher would probably drop in for a visit. It would take less time just to answer.

She picked up the receiver just before the tenth ring. Her voice cracked. "Hello?"

"Phoebe? Are you okay?" It was Jonathan Long, her husband's friend and business partner.

Phoebe felt her stomach constrict. She should have ignored the call: she didn't need him and Marge telling her what she should do. For David's sake, though, she had to be polite. Duty.

"Oh, yes, I'm fine. David's relatives just left, so I was resting."

"Sorry to disturb you, but Marge had an idea. Here, I'll let her talk to you."

Marge's brisk voice came over the line. "How are you holding up, dear?"

"Pretty well now that everyone's finally gone."

"You must be lonely. How would you like a dog?"

"A dog?"

"Yeah, a dog. They can be such good company, always cheerful and ready to please. It's just what you need to keep you company in that empty house."

Phoebe was silent. Trust 'Marge the Organizer' to strike quickly. Why did she think she should decide what was good for other people! Usually I go along with her, just to avoid hurting her feelings because she and Jon have been friends of ours for so many years. But I really don't want to cater to anyone else right now, especially not a puppy. I'm going to have to stay strong against Marge's determination this time.

"Phoebe? Are you there?"

"Yes," she replied. "I just haven't thought...."

"Yes, yes, of course, I realize it's hard to think ahead, but life must go on, you know. You've got to keep your time occupied. You know how I worry about you."

"Thank you, but I'm doing fine. Maybe at some...."

"Fine!" Marge's enthusiastic voice boomed through the receiver.

Phoebe pulled away and missed Marge's next words. She said, "I'm sorry I didn't hear what you said."

"Do you need anything?"

"Not a thing. I've got so much food that I can't eat it all before it spoils. Why don't you two come over to help me eat some of it tomorrow evening?" The words slipped out before she realized what she was saying.

"Let me check with Jonathan."

A silence at the other end stretched on for several moments. Ah, they can't come, they have other plans. Phoebe congratulated herself on safely observing the amenities without consequence.

Marge's voice came back on the line. "We're free. What time would you like us?"

"Six o'clock." Another automatic response. For thirty-nine years, David had insisted dinner be on the table promptly at six. She could change that, too, if she worked at it.

After hanging up, she tried to figure out how she had managed to saddle herself with company when all she wanted was to be alone. Old habits certainly died hard. The two couples had spent many evenings together playing cards and sharing meals she cooked. Phoebe had decided that, with David gone, she would do as she pleased for the first time in fifty years. First it had been her mother ordering her around, then her husband.

She spent the rest of the afternoon washing bed linens and towels. Precisely at five o'clock she found herself headed for the kitchen to begin preparing a meal. When she reached the doorway, Phoebe stopped suddenly. No one else was expecting to eat at a specific time. She could break the pattern right now and start doing as she pleased. Deliberately she turned around and went into her laundry room to fold and put away clean linens. She was ravenous when she sat down to eat after seven o'clock. While cleaning up the kitchen, she chose leftovers for the following evening. As she turned out the kitchen light, the clock in the living room chimed nine—bedtime.

"So much for my leisurely evening," Phoebe mumbled. She checked that the front door was locked and started up the stairway. She stopped on the third step.

"Who says I have to go to bed now? Or that I have to get up at five o'clock?"

She turned around and headed for the den. For the first time in many years, she turned on all the lights in the room: the one on the ceiling, the desk lamp, and the pole lamp next to her corner of the sofa. Half expecting to hear David's voice saying, "Think about the electric bill," she stayed strong, determined to have enough light to read.

She scanned the wall of books, six shelves from floor to ceiling. Because David had arranged the books alphabetically by author, not type, she had trouble finding anything she wanted to read when she had a few spare minutes. She could never remember authors' names, just knew what kind of book she was in the mood for. How could she find a mystery sandwiched between an autobiography and an economics text? She would rearrange the shelves the way she wanted, maybe even give away those that didn't interest her. But not tonight. Tonight she'd settle for the adventure story she had taken to him when he was in the hospital. She finally found it in the unpacked bag she had brought home, along with his wallet, dentures, eyeglasses, and clothing. She'd have to do something about them, but not tonight.

Phoebe curled up in her corner of the sofa and lost herself in the world of speeding cars, loose women, and smart investigators. She wasn't aware of the time until she reached the last line. With the book closed on her lap, savoring the ingenious plot, she heard the clock chime.

"One, two, three," she counted automatically, then sat bolt upright. "Goodness, look at the time!" She got up and set the book on the corner of the desk, promising herself to rearrange the books soon.

Climbing into bed, she caught herself pulling out the pin to set the alarm clock. She slapped her wrist and pushed the pin back in before turning out the light. It was the height of luxury to spread across the whole double bed. She fell asleep, with thoughts of a handsome detective chasing the bad guys with her by his side.

Phoebe awoke the next morning with a start, worried that she'd overslept. Looking at the luminous dial, she saw it was six o'clock. She came fully awake but then sank back onto her pillow when she remembered the empty space next to her. There was no one expecting an early breakfast this morning. However, try as she might, she couldn't go back to sleep.

"Well, I may as well get up," she said to the alarm clock. Despite the short night, she actually felt rested—no elbows or knees poked into her at sporadic intervals while she slept, no massive arms thrown into her face in sleepy spasms. A whole day spread before her, with no relatives to please.

The day passed rapidly. Phoebe finished writing her thank-you notes and started boxing up David's clothes for the consignment shop. She made a list of David's things to give away—his briefcase to Jonathan, his bowling bag and ball to the local boys' club, books she didn't want to the library. The day sped by without any time to read. All too soon it was time to warm up the donated food she had set aside. The doorbell rang just before six o'clock. When Phoebe opened the door, she saw her guests had not come empty handed. Marge held a large paper sack and Jonathan balanced a cardboard box with both hands.

"You shouldn't have brought anything," Phoebe protested. "I have lots of food."

Marge laughed. "Oh, this isn't for us," she said pushing past Phoebe. "Show her what you have there, Jon."

Her husband followed Marge into the kitchen and set the box on the floor. He motioned for Phoebe to come closer. When she did, Phoebe stared at a ball of white fluff curled up in one corner of the box.

"What is it?" she asked.

"It's a puppy, silly," replied Marge. "And I've got everything right here that you'll need for a couple of days, even a book on care and feeding." She began pulling out smaller bags from her sack, now on the kitchen counter.

Phoebe was speechless. The buzzer on the oven saved her from having to say anything except, "Dinner's ready."

"I fed the puppy just before we left, so we should be able to eat before he wakes up," Marge said as she spread out her remaining gifts on the counter. "We can sort through this later. I see you've already set the dining room table. Let Jon pour the wine, and I'll set out the serving dishes."

As usual when Marge came to visit, she immediately took charge, while Phoebe followed her friend's directions. As the three of them began eating, small talk accompanied the casserole of vegetables and unknown meat for several minutes. Then a sharp yip came from the kitchen.

Marge jumped up. "Oh, he's awake."

Before Phoebe could react, Marge returned with the ball of fluff and dumped it in her hostess's lap. A sturdy red leash miraculously appeared, and Marge thrust the looped handle toward Phoebe.

"The first thing you learn is to take him outside as soon as he wakes up, so that he doesn't have an accident inside the house. I'll start the coffee and clear the plates while you take him outside. Is that apple pie in the fridge for us?"

Phoebe nodded. She found herself carrying the soft, warm body out the back door to set it on a patch of grass. The puppy immediately began sniffing around the new scene and within a few minutes squatted down successfully. Although Phoebe tugged gently at the leash, the puppy had other ideas, wanting to explore all the new smells.

Marge called from the doorway, "Did you two got lost? Coffee's ready."

Tugging and calling, Phoebe gradually persuaded her new responsibility to return inside. She gritted her teeth and resolved she wouldn't let this intruder be her boss. She unsnapped the leash and placed the puppy back in the box. Returning to her guests, she found them well into their dessert and coffee.

Jonathan asked, "Have you decided on a name?"

Phoebe hesitated. "No, not yet. I don't really want...."

As soon as she started speaking, a furious yipping arose in the kitchen.

Marge chuckled. "I think she already knows her mommy's voice. What a baby! Say, how about that for a name?"

"Well, I don't know,"

"Unless you have a better idea, Baby's a good choice. You can't call her 'dog,' now can you?"

Phoebe sighed in frustration at trying to hold back the juggernaut named Marge. People expected the two of them to be best friends because their husbands were partners and the two couples socialized regularly. David expected the same thing because he and Jonathan had been friends since boyhood. Whenever the wives went shopping together, Marge was the one who led the way into the stores. When they ate lunch at a restaurant, Marge chose the location. Phoebe had found it easier to roll along in the wake of the storm than to do battle over every decision. Between them, her husband and Marge had made most of her decisions for many years. It was more peaceful that way. Phoebe wished it could be different. Maybe with David gone, she could change.

After that, shrill yipping woke Phoebe twice every night and early every morning, usually before five o'clock. It seemed to be a continuous sound whenever Baby wasn't napping. During the day, Baby took short naps, giving Phoebe just enough time to start a chore before the puppy woke up and insisted on attention. For bedtime reading, Phoebe started the book on dog care that Marge had provided. It corroborated Marge's advice to anticipate the puppy's needs but didn't cover training the dog rather than the owner.

Phoebe discovered that Baby didn't like to be cooped up in the box all day. The puppy gave no obvious signs when it needed to go outside. Because she didn't want to risk having her carpets ruined, Phoebe watched it like a predator looking for a meal, watching for that slight motion that meant it was time to move. There was a new boss in her house. Could she insist that Marge take back the dog? Knowing that would be ungrateful, Phoebe decided to keep trying to adjust.

During the next few weeks, Phoebe's eyes developed dark circles. She stumbled out of bed to take Baby outside first thing in the morning, fed her, and played with her. Sometimes she managed to doze off while Baby napped, only to begin all over again when the puppy woke up.

The books were still in alphabetical order and unread. Phoebe fell behind in her housekeeping for the first time in her adult life. She could write her name in the dust, and dirty dishes were stacked in the sink. Phoebe managed to vacuum, while Baby barked and chased the moving nozzle. That was fun, but not enough to make up for all the other inconveniences. One time Baby got underfoot and Phoebe would have fallen if she hadn't grabbed hold of a nearby chair. When she yelled at the dog for nearly causing serious injury, Baby nervously sent a stream of urine across a parquet floor. After that, Phoebe sighed whenever she felt herself getting irritated.

During her marriage, Phoebe had kept her house clean and comfortable, taking pride in satisfying her husband's demands for perfect housekeeping. She had baked homemade pies and cakes, ironed her husband's clothes including underwear, sewed her own clothes and mended his. At the same time, she longed for all the unread books, all the undiscovered adventures waiting for her. How free those days seemed now, for she had managed to squeeze in at least a few hours of reading each day. These days she never seemed to have any time for herself and was deprived of a good night's sleep.

To Marge's inquiries about the puppy, Phoebe gave noncommittal responses. When she took the puppy to the veterinarian for a series of immunizations, he told her Baby was an expensive Bishon Friese. She agreed when she saw the bills. Trying to return the dog to Marge would be an ungracious thing for her to do, and Phoebe always did the right thing.

Phoebe felt trapped, even more than she had under her husband's demands for perfection and punctuality. At least then she had finished her chores and salvaged a little time for herself. Baby never left her side. The puppy never criticized or complained, but it was always there.

About a month after the puppy's arrival, Phoebe dragged herself out of bed one morning, pulled on her bathrobe and slippers, and hurried downstairs in response to Baby's yipping. With the leash attached to the puppy's collar, Phoebe carried it to the back door, opened the door, and stopped. Several inches of snow lay on the ground. She couldn't go outside in her cloth slippers. Baby began to squirm and bark furiously.

Phoebe tried setting it on the porch. Even when she stretched as far as she could, Baby was still on the bottom step, pulling hard on its leash. Worried that the puppy might hurt itself, Phoebe let go.

Baby catapulted off the last step and into the snow. It rolled with delight in the new sensation, finally squatting in a flattened area of snow.

"Good girl. Come, Baby. Come to Mommy," called Phoebe, starting to shiver in the open doorway.

Baby wagged a plumy tail, tongue hanging out, but came no closer.

Phoebe stooped in the doorway and reached out. "Please, Baby, it's cold. Come."

Baby stood fast, the red leash trailing behind in the snow.

Phoebe called again, more insistently, but without success. "Well, you little scamp, if that's the way you want it, that's the way it is."

She turned around, went back into the house, and slammed the door. Then she looked out the kitchen window to see what effect this had on the puppy. Baby stood in the same spot, staring at the door.

Grumbling, Phoebe stomped up the stairs and got dressed, checking all the closets for her boots. It took her more than fifteen minutes to find them in a box of mittens and caps under the cellar stairway. As she pulled them on, the front doorbell rang. Outside stood a somber-faced boy about twelve years old with a newspaper bag slung over one shoulder and a limp white ball of fluff in his arms. Phoebe didn't at first recognize what it was.

"Ma'am, is this your dog?"

Outwardly calm, she nodded, while inside she felt a pang of regret. The little dog had been a nuisance, but it didn't deserve to be hurt or worse.

The boy tried hard to blink back tears. "Oh, ma'am, I'm so sorry. I was just coming down the street when I saw this little white thing run out into the street. It dashed out right in front of an oil truck. The driver didn't slow down; he didn't know he'd hit anything. I was too shook up to look at the license plate. I tried to wake the puppy but he's hurt. What can I do?"

"Oh, dear," Phoebe replied slowly. "The puppy ran out the door before I was dressed and wouldn't come when I called. I guess it was excited because it never saw snow before. How bad is it?" Her voice trailed off.

The boy shifted his bag slightly. "I think we, I mean you, need to take her to a vet. I got to finish my route and get to school."

"Of course. Well, thank you for taking the time to tell me about it."

"No problem, ma'am." He hesitated. "Would you like me to go along with you?"

"I'll be fine. You shouldn't miss school."

The boy grinned. "There's a field trip today to the art museum, and art's not really my thing. I'd be glad to go with you. This poor little girl needs a lot of attention."

Just then Baby whimpered softly. Phoebe felt hope that the puppy would survive.

"I don't want you to get into trouble," said Phoebe. "Your mother will be worried."

The boy stood up straighter. "I'm a boy scout and I'm supposed to help people. I think you need help. I have to call my mom, though."

"Well, let's get moving then. By the way, I'm Mrs. Hardy. What's your name?"

"Jack, Jack Higgins."

With Jack sitting in the back seat holding the box with the puppy, Phoebe drove to the office of the veterinarian who had given Baby her shots. While Phoebe waited with the boy during the examination, Jack kept jiggling his leg.

"Do you think she'll be all right?" he finally asked.

"The doctor has an excellent reputation. Do you have a dog of your own?"

Jack shook his head. "Not yet. I've been saving up my paper route money, cuz Mom says if I want a dog, I have to pay for the dog food and other stuff."

Phoebe had an inspiration. Could she dare to go behind Marge's back and give away such a very generous gift? Knowing what a drain on her energy it was to care for such an energetic puppy, Phoebe resolved that she could be strong—as long as she kept the sound of Baby's insistent yipping in front of her.

Diagnosis of two broken legs and some internal bleeding meant the puppy had to stay at least overnight. Phoebe drove Jack to his home and asked to come in to speak with his mother.

"You can be very proud of your son," Phoebe began. "He acted very responsibly when he found my injured puppy."

Mrs. Higgins smiled. "Yes, he's very reliable for a ten-year-old."

Phoebe cleared her throat. "I've been having difficulty in caring for such an energetic dog."

The other woman glanced at her son. "It's like raising a child."

"Exactly," replied Phoebe. "It takes someone with energy and a sense of responsibility. Reliability is another good quality."

Jack suddenly sat up. "I told you, Mom, that I can take care of a dog."

Phoebe made her decision. "Mrs. Higgins, I'll pay for the vet bills, but I would be more than happy to turn over the puppy for Jack to train and raise."

"Oh, Mom, can I? Can I?"

So Baby found a new home, and Phoebe had time to catch up on her household chores. She washed the stack of dishes in the sink and got out the vacuum to do a thorough cleaning. It was nearly three days later before she had the house in its previously neat state.

Then she sat down to enjoy a leisurely cup of tea, enjoying the peace and quiet. The house did suddenly seem very silent. She turned on the radio, just for the noise.

Then the telephone rang. It was Marge.

"How are you and Baby doing?" asked the brisk voice.

"Oh, dear," stammered Phoebe. "There's been an accident."

"Are you hurt?"

"I'm fine but the puppy ran out the door before I was dressed to go out in the snow. She wouldn't come when I called and ran off. Then she got hit by a truck, and the driver never stopped." Phoebe took a breath. "She's badly hurt, but the vet fixed her up as good as new."

"You must be overwhelmed with nursing her. I'll be over as soon as I can."

"That's nice of you," replied Phoebe, "but she isn't here."

"Oh, you mean she's still with the vet?"

Phoebe took a deep breath. "No, she has a new home."

There was no response. Could it be that Marge had nothing to say?

Phoebe plunged ahead. "You and Jonathan were so good to think of me being lonely. But I'm not ready to care for someone new in my life just yet."

"Oh." Marge actually sounded contrite.

"I appreciate the thought, really I do." Phoebe took a deep breath. "Please don't try to anticipate my needs. I don't know myself what they'll be."

"I think I understand." A sigh came across the line. "I don't know what I'd do if anything happened to Jon."

Phoebe smiled to herself. Maybe Marge could understand Phoebe's side. Aloud, she said, "I need some time to figure out what I want. Perhaps in the future I'll decide my house is too quiet and I'll get a dog."

"Just let me know when you're ready and I'll…"

"Yes, I know you want to go with me to choose one. Thank you for your thoughtfulness, but I really need to start making decisions on my own."

A Fleeting Glimpse

Knitting Circle with Gun

It's Wednesday afternoon at Sylvia's house, time for the weekly meeting of the WOLF club. The six regular members settle themselves in the small living room, balancing tea cups and bags of knitting.

Sylvia, a redhead today, waits for the clink of stirring spoons to stop and the click of knitting needles to begin.

She asks, "So, Pauline, did you get the gun?"

Knitting needles stop. Five pairs of eyes stare at the woman whose feet cannot reach the floor from the smaller of two pale blue, upholstered chairs.

Pauline's head is permanently bent so far forward that her shoulders sit a mere four inches below the top of it. Today she wears one of her cotton print dresses, covered with a ragged cardigan. She stills the slow, deliberate movements of her misshapen fingers, bent into impossible angles from arthritis, and leans back in the chair to turn her neck, the only way she can look at the others. In a surprisingly strong voice, she replies, "It's under the yarn in my bag."

A collective sigh is barely audible as knitting needles resume working on the brown and gray and tan of church yarn that is slowly becoming hats and scarves.

"Good," says Sylvia, consulting a creased, yellowed paper in her hand. She sits alone on a love seat, originally a bright red and blue floral design on a beige background. Her brown slacks and sweater are only slightly darker than the present colors of the upholstery.

"Point of order!" calls out a slight woman at a small writing desk, who has pulled out a pen and paper pad. She clears her throat and straightens her black-rimmed glasses. "You haven't called the meeting to order yet, Madame Chairman."

"Thank you, Norma." Sylvia raps three times with her knuckles on the rectangular coffee table. "The weekly meeting of the Women of Limited Finances will please come to order."

A gray-haired woman in a stained blue sweat suit stops knitting and rocking to raise her hand.

"The chair recognizes Hilda."

"I move that we dispense with the reading of the minutes from last week, since we were all here and should remember what went on, unless someone developed Alzheimer's since then!"

A ripple of laughter passes around the room. Sylvia again raps on the coffee table. "Order, please, ladies. I need a second to the motion."

A woman in black whose hips cover more than half of a wooden bench along one wall replies, "I'll second."

"Thank you, Emma. All in favor?"

A chorus of "Aye" follows quickly. Norma sniffs audibly, then adjusts her glasses and writes on the pad. Sylvia scratches a spot on the back of her neck, moving the red wig slightly askew so that a single wisp of dingy hair escapes next to her left ear. She squints at the paper in her hand.

"It's time for the money," reminds an angular woman on the second pale blue armchair. This armchair, however, seems a miniature since the woman's knees are almost to her chin and her strip of brown and tan knitting stretches to the floor and halfway over to the coffee table.

"That's right, Madeline, thanks," agrees Sylvia. "Treasurer's report. Emma?"

The obese woman in black pulls a bank book from her knitting bag. She lumbers to her feet, swaying slightly at first. "Um, we've got sixty-seven dollars and forty-nine cents as of yesterday. Friday we'll get some interest. Any bills? Any contributions?" She looks up hopefully as she finishes.

"I got another two thirty-five for bottles and cans," says Pauline, struggling to pull a change purse out of her sweater pocket. Madeline stands up, bending almost in half to stoop over and help her friend. While the two of them struggle to disentangle the pocket, Hilda and Sylvia hand Emma several coins each.

"Anyone else?" asks Emma, looking pointedly at Norma's back. "Thanks, Madeline." She pauses. "Norma? Anything?"

The slim woman at the desk sits up straight but doesn't look at the others. Her voice is barely audible. "Nothing this week. I ran out of food."

Knitting needles click furiously and a few tea cups rattle. Emma clears her throat. "That gives us seventy-one dollars and thirty-seven cents. Dues from next week's social security checks should bring us close to our budgeted income."

"Don't forget the money Pauline has to give Frankie," says Madeline, stretching her long legs across the open area of the grayish carpet. "He doesn't like to wait for his money."

"Right," says Emma, concentrating on her scrap of paper. "I'll go to the bank first thing in the morning and bring over the fifty dollars…."

"Uh, it's sixty," says Pauline in a clear voice, concentrating on the gray stitches in her lap.

After a short silence, Emma says, "But we budgeted fifty, and you said Frankie agreed."

"It's not Pauline's fault," Madeline answers, glaring at the others while her hands create a staccato with the aluminum needles. "Frankie says it's harder to find a gun that can't be traced. He needs an extra ten for his trouble."

Norma clears her throat. "Point of order."

"The chair recognizes Norma." Sylvia scratches vigorously under her wig.

Norma stands up straight, barely five feet two. "I think we need to vote on amending the budget. After all, we allocated a specific amount for expenses at the beginning. Being on limited incomes, with some of us barely able to feed ourselves, we can't just find extra money all of a sudden."

Hilda stops rocking and starts speaking without Sylvia's permission. "And what about the schedule? If we aren't ready, we have to wait until next year's tag sale at the church to get rid of the disguises. I say we need the gun, and we need it now. We can't give it back. So we just have to figure out how to make up the extra ten dollars."

"Uh, it's actually an extra thirty," interposes Pauline, making no attempt to raise her bent head to look at the group. "Frankie says if we want bullets, it'll be an extra five dollars for each one, and we figured we need four."

Excited chatter drowns out any noise of knitting needles or tea cups. Sylvia raps her knuckles on the coffee table, but no one pays any attention to her. Finally, she grabs her teaspoon and bangs on the wooden table top.

"Ladies! Please contain yourselves. Yes, Hilda?"

"Since we can't find extra money, can't we cut back on the number of bullets?"

Emma raises her hand and begins speaking before Sylvia acknowledges her. "But we decided that I need two to get their attention and two more to scare anyone who tries to stop us. I don't think we can cut back in that area."

"Well, then, how about cutting down on the brownie expense? Perhaps once a month instead?" asks Hilda, placidly setting her rocking chair in motion to match the movement of her hands and needles.

Madeline stands up, her nearly six feet towering over the group. "I object to any such idea. Rick expects his weekly batch of brownies in exchange for teaching me how to survive in the projects. I'm just about ready to ask about hot-wiring a car, but if we change our plans and go back on my agreement, our schedule will really get messed up."

She glares at Hilda, who shrugs and looks down, pretending to salvage a dropped stitch.

"Besides," Madeline continues, "you're safe enough in that trailer park. Since I started exchanging brownies for information, I haven't been mugged at all, and Pauline's been robbed only once." She sits down again, careful to avoid impaling herself on her metal knitting needles.

Sylvia scratches the back of her head. By now the red wig is nearly down to her eyebrows. She looks up and sighs. "Any suggestions?"

"Point of order."

Without looking at the speaker, Sylvia sighs and says, "Yes, Norma?"

"I think we should vote on the treasurer's report before voting on approving the increased expense. That's really new business."

"Fine. Do I have a motion to accept the treasurer's report of...what was the balance again, Emma?"

The large woman consults her notes. "Seventy-one thirty-seven."

Hilda doesn't miss a beat of her rocking or knitting. "I move we accept the treasurer's report."

Madeline says, "Second."

Sylvia barely says, "All in favor," before the women chorus "Aye."

"Now, where were we?" muses Sylvia, squinting at the paper yet again.

"Old business," says Hilda.

"Correspondence," insists Norma, furiously writing.

Sylvia looks up. "Anyone receive any correspondence?"

"Yeah, I got an offer of a million dollars again," says Hilda. "I'd be a multi-millionaire by now if they were real. Then we wouldn't have to rob the bank."

"Only correspondence directly applicable to this group's purpose is admissible in the minutes," insists Norma, glaring across the room.

"No correspondence, fine," says Sylvia quickly. "So I guess we go on to old business. Where do we stand on supplies? Hilda, I think that's your department."

The chunky woman deliberately rolls up her partly finished brown scarf and stands up in front of the rocking chair. "Everything's on time and within budget, as my ex used to say." She pauses as if waiting for laughter, then proceeds when none is forthcoming. "Emma and I've been sorting clothes the rich folks at church are bringing in for the tag sale on December seventh. So far we found nearly all the men's shoes we need. There's a shortage of men's clothes being discarded this year, so we still have a way to go. Pauline has helped with extras from the trash bins she searches, especially large plastic shopping bags with handles. Emma and I thought those would be perfect for collecting the disguises afterwards."

Several gray-haired heads nod in agreement while knitting needles continue to move in a relentless rhythm.

Sylvia frowns. "I may still have some of Jacob's clothes...."

Madeline interrupts. "Now, dear, you know we can't use them. We have to make sure everything we discard can't be traced directly to any of us. Besides, we still have four weeks."

Sylvia nods. "Who else has a report?"

Norma coughs lightly. "We haven't heard about transportation."

"Oh, yes," agrees Sylvia, squinting at the yellowed paper. "Madeline, have you arranged for a get-away car?"

The tall woman nods. "The church parking lot continues to attract the usual supply of abandoned cars. There was a beautiful white Mercedes last week, but I saw Rick take it away yesterday."

"Nondescript, Madeline," insists Norma. "Remember, the car must be ordinary, dirty, too, if possible."

Madeline sighs and nods in agreement. "I know, but I can dream, can't I? There's a gray Escort been there for a few days that's probably perfect. Either it doesn't run or no one's interested in Ford parts. Nope, I don't think the car will pose a problem as long as I can learn how to start it." She winks. "Just keep those brownies coming."

"Okay. We seem to be making progress." Sylvia glances at the paper in her hand. "Is there any new business? Norma?"

"We need to discuss the extra expense for the gun and the bullets. Unless we resolve it, we won't have money to put gas in the car Madeline finds."

Sylvia sighs. "Anyone have an idea? Yes, Madeline?"

"I move that we pay Frankie for the gun now and for the bullets later, as we get the extra money."

"Second," says Pauline quickly.

Everyone again agrees. Silence then fills the room.

"I hesitate to ask, but does anyone have any ideas about how we can make some extra money?" Sylvia sounds more firmly now.

Madeline looks up with a grim smile. "We could sell some of these hats and scarves we're making."

A different chorus, less agreeable, meets her suggestion.

Norma voices their objections. "But the yarn isn't ours. The church gave it to us so we could make warm accessories for the homeless this winter. We can't sell them!"

Madeline shrugs and looks down at the motionless needles in her hands. "It was just an idea."

"At least someone is trying to solve the problem," says Sylvia in a placating voice. "I recommend that our priority until next week's meeting is to think about ways to find the extra money we need. Agreed?"

Heads nod and a few voices mumble "Okay."

Sylvia consults her paper. "That seems to be all the business I have on the agenda. Does anyone see any major problems with meeting our target date of November twenty-third?"

No one disagrees.
"Does everyone understand what they need to do before next week?"
Heads nod.
"Then this meeting is adjourned. Anyone for more tea?"

K. E. Swope

Leaf Battle

Dick Pincus raked leaves and grumbled. "My red maple, his pin oak, my sugar maple, his red oak." He looked up and glared at the ranch-style house across the driveway.

This fall had started out the same as all the others. At the first sign of the trees changing color, Dick checked his three rakes—heavy-duty plastic for the busiest part of the season, fine-toothed balsa-wood for small leaf fragments, and lightweight plastic for the rest. Several years ago he had yelled at his wife when she used his balsa rake to gather debris from her tomato plot. Since then, she agreed to keep the inside of the house tidy and allowed him to manicure their yard to his own standards.

Until last year Dick's fall task had been easier. His nearest neighbor, Joe, had been just as conscientious in raking regularly. He and Dick had taken breaks at the same time, meeting in the driveway to talk. But Joe had sold the house and moved to Florida last October, just as the leaves were in full color and the early raining of leaves began. The new owner didn't have the same pride in keeping his yard clear, hiring a local lawn service instead. Dick could accept that, but he couldn't accept that the lazy sod waited until his trees were bare. By that time Dick figured more than half those oak leaves had blown across the driveway and he had bagged them along with his own.

His wife wouldn't take the problem seriously. Of course, she didn't have to rake the leaves. One night she had said, "If it makes you so angry, you could rake Mr. Mandeville's oak leaves into a separate pile and dump them back in his yard."

Women! What a stupid idea—the prevailing winds would blow them back and he'd have to rake them up a second time. Added to that was having to pay to get rid of them. As of last year the town no longer picked up leaves along with the trash collection, to save taxpayer money, they said. And no leaf burning was allowed. He had paid someone a fortune to haul away eighty-seven leaf bags last year. Since his retirement, he resented spending money on someone else's leaves.

His wife had suggested he ask Mr. Mandeville to pay part of the cost. How could he knock on a stranger's door to ask for money? "Hi, I'm your neighbor Dick Pincus and I want fifty dollars because your leaves blow into my yard and I have to get rid of them."

It would be different if the jerk stuck his head out of doors once in a while so Dick could casually introduce himself and get to know him. Probably addicted to TV, one of those couch potatoes who wouldn't think for themselves. His wife had to agree that the new neighbor was less than friendly. She had tried to make him welcome to the neighborhood. He had opened the door when she knocked, but hadn't invited her in nor had he encouraged a lengthy conversation. She hadn't tried again.

So Dick raked and grumbled. He thought about ways to separate out the oak leaves and dump them back into his neighbor's yard after dark in some way so the wind wouldn't blow them back to him. He'd probably have to glue them there, not very practical. Suddenly the words 'after dark' gave him an idea.

Somewhere in the storage loft of the garage was an old Radio Flyer wagon with high sides. Although covered in layers of dust, it needed just a little oil on the wheels to be useful. His wife shook her head and went back to her sewing.

Six full leaf bags stood upright in the bed of the wagon, held in place by the high sides. Then Dick waited for dark. He didn't want anyone to see him.

At ten o'clock, when most of the people on the street were watching the news, Dick put his plan into action. He pulled the loaded wagon out of his garage, out the driveway, and down the hill to the cul-de-sac on his dead-end street. The well-oiled wheels rolled smoothly, although the hard rubber gradually crumbled and fell away. Soon there was no rubber left on the wheels and the wooden disks rumbled over the paving. Dick watched windows on both sides of the street for faces investigating the unusual noise, but everyone seemed too engrossed in TV to notice the wagon passing. He didn't think dumping his leaves on the vacant lot at the end of the street was against the law. He just didn't want his neighbors to laugh at him. It was so simple, except when the wagon tried to race him to the bottom of the hill.

Once he reached the overgrown double lot, he scattered the leaves among the brush. The wind couldn't blow them back to his yard now, it was too far away. He folded the bags to use them again and returned home, pleased with his resourcefulness.

Six bags that first night, four more later that week. By the end of October leaves came raining down, a cloudburst of nature's castoff glory. Dick soon needed four trips a week, because the darn oak leaves took up twice as much space as his own dainty maples, no matter how hard he stomped and stomped to pack each bag.

One evening, he had fourteen bags to cart away, two loads if he took seven at once to save time. Six stood upright on the Radio Flyer as usual, with the last lying sideways on top. With his left hand balancing the bag on top, Dick walked backwards and used his right hand to pull the loaded wagon. Every minute or so he looked ahead over his shoulder to check that the path was clear and he was heading straight.

Perhaps he was in too much of a hurry. Perhaps he tripped on a stone in the dark. Just as he reached the steepest part of his downhill path, the bag lying on top slipped. He let go of the wagon handle to grab the bag before the leaves spewed out all over the road. Unfortunately, he held the bag's bottom and leaves fell out anyway. Meanwhile, the wagon started rolling away. Dick dropped the bag and ran after the wagon. Before he could catch it, the wagon hit the curbing. Then it stopped, with its six upright bags half empty. Leaves covered the road, mostly the larger oak ones.

Dick looked around to see if anyone had noticed the wagon's wild ride. "Damn leaves," he grumbled. He stalked back to his garage to retrieve his heavy plastic rake.

Dick's wife came out when she heard the garage door open. "Oh, it's you, dear," she said. "Where's your carriage?"

"Don't ask." He stomped out the driveway carrying the rake like a rifle.

He set up the nearly empty bag that had caused him all this trouble. By the light of a nearby streetlight, he began to rake up leaves from the road.

A tall shadow separated itself from what had appeared to be a fat telephone pole. Dick let go of the bag he was steadying. The leaves he had just raked fell out onto the street.

"What are you doing?" asked a muffled voice. Nearly upon him, the apparition displayed a gaping hole, snow white, where its mouth should be.

Dick's first instinct was to run. Nothing mortal should be lurking in the shadows this late at night. Dick raised the rake across his body, a poor excuse for the cross that priests used to deter vampires.

Backing up slowing but keeping the rake between him and his assailant, Dick said, "What...who are you?"

Dick backed up farther—and fell over the bag of leaves.

A hollow laugh was the response. Dick closed his eyes, waiting for the end.

The muffled voice said, "Do you need help?"

Dick opened one eye. Looming over him was a man, but a man like none he had ever seen before. The white gash across the middle of what must be a face had no fangs dripping blood. It was just white emptiness. Deep sockets under bushy eyebrows probably held eyes, but they were unseen in the dark. If he survived this, Dick vowed to lobby for more streetlights. He closed his eye again. He felt an ache in his chest. He began to pant.

"Are you hurt?" The voice, though not clear, sounded kindly.

Dick tried to take a deep breath, but the ache intensified. He forced his eyes open.

A gloved hand reached out.

Dick recoiled. Through clenched teeth he asked, "Who the hell are you?" His voice sounded weak rather than angry as intended.

Again the voice sounded kind. "I'm Sam Mandeville. I was out for a walk and heard this strange rumble, so I came down the street to investigate."

Dick tried to get up but found his legs wouldn't answer his wish. "You! It's all your fault that…." He sank back, finding he had no breath left to continue.

A Fleeting Glimpse

"I'm sorry I startled you and caused you to trip."

"That's not what I meant." Dick gasped for breath before he could continue. "If you raked up your damn leaves like everyone else...." He ran out of breath before he could finish.

"Excuse me? My leaves?"

"Yes, your damn leaves blow into MY yard! Then I have to pay to have your leaves hauled away." That's all Dick could get out before he had to stop to breathe.

The head far above Dick turned from side to side, as if seeing the scene in a fresh light. "And so you chose to dump them at the end of the street."

"Now you're here," Dick started but had to pause to breathe, "you can finish."

"I'm afraid that's impossible."

Dick groaned at the flash of pain that hit him across his shoulder blades. "Impossible?" He tried to shout but it came out as a whisper. "Why in bloody hell can't you take care of your own damn leaves?"

He couldn't hear the answer. His head started sinking down on his chest, dragged down by a pull he couldn't resist. He thought he was being pushed, pulled, and generally dragged into the wagon. Then it flew through the air behind a tall, black figure to his house. In a fog, he heard the sirens. Then he lost consciousness completely.

The next thing Dick was aware of was the color white. White ceiling, white walls, white curtains, white covers on the bed where he lay. Then he noticed tubes, like rubbery worms crawling into his nose, his mouth, even his wrists.

"Hello, dear," said his wife's voice. She was sitting on a chair next to the bed.

"What happened?" Dick knew that's what he said, but it wasn't what his ears heard.

She smiled with her lips but not her eyes. "You had a heart attack. It was lucky that Mr. Mandeville found you and brought you home.'

Dick suddenly remembered the apparition. "Mandeville?"

"Yes, dear. Even though it jeopardized his own health, he managed to pull you up the hill to the house, and I called the ambulance. They brought both of you in together."

"Why?"

"It seems that poor man has such extreme allergies, he can only leave his house if he wears a filter over his mouth and nose. And then he only ventures out at night to avoid the worst of the allergens."

Dick snorted. "Filter?"

"You know, like a surgeon's mask."

Dick remembered the apparition's white gash in place of a mouth.

His wife continued. "That's why he doesn't rake his own leaves—he can't. It makes too much dust. Most of the year he's practically a prisoner in his own house."

Dick was quiet for a minute. "How do you know so much about it?"

"Oh, I stopped in to thank him. He's in a room downstairs, on oxygen. They admitted him because he overexerted himself pulling you up the hill." She hesitated. "He said he'd like to come up to visit you, once you feel up to it."

Dick grunted. "Why?"

"Since he can't be outdoors or stop the wind from blowing, he says he'd like to work out a way to pay part of the cost of leaf disposal."

Dick grunted again. He tried to nod in agreement, but suddenly he felt very sleepy. Maybe they could work something out. And maybe not. But first he'd have to give that joker a piece of his mind for scaring him.

Neighborly

Jane Moseby paused, key in hand, ready to unlock the door to her room in Miss Millicent's Home for Widows. Scuffling noises were coming from behind the door across the hallway. Susan's funeral had been nearly a week ago, and no one from her family had attended. Now it seemed that someone was finally taking an interest in her, even if it was only the things she left behind.

Putting her key in her pocket, Jane drifted across the frayed carpet in the hallway. The door wasn't latched, just pushed nearly shut. She opened the door a bit further, enough to see into the room. Sure enough, half a dozen corrugated boxes stood on the floor beside the single bed, flaps still open. Whoever was inside wasn't nearly finished packing up. Perhaps they'd like some help, she thought. And perhaps she'd finally get to see someone from the family Susan never talked about.

Jane took one step into the room and stopped short. A bulky man, brown as cinnamon, was packing up Susan's things. All the residents of the home were pale white, since their skin tended to lighten and glisten as they aged. Except for the midnight black of the Haitian maids and the deep tan of the dining room stewards from Dominican Republic, rarely did any people of color other than white enter the lives of the ladies.

Clearing her throat, Jane said, "Hello."

Startled, the man nearly dropped the mug he was wrapping in newsprint. He caught it before it fell, showing dexterity not obvious from his size. He grunted, finished wrapping up the mug and placed it in a box next to the desk. Ignoring the visitor, he picked up an alarm clock and another piece of newsprint.

"Would you like some help?" Jane didn't give up easily.

"Not much here. I can handle it," he replied without looking up.

Undeterred, Jane tried again. "I know. It's the curse of old age. We seem to shed our possessions almost as fast as we lose our friends."

This time he looked at her directly. A wide smile split his face, revealing sparkling, perfect white teeth. "Sorry. If you don't mind doing the clothes, I'd appreciate it. I never did master the knack of folding clothes to prevent wrinkles."

"My name's Jane. Susan and I were neighbors since she moved in."

"I'm Clarence." He made no motion to shake hands but continued wrapping the alarm clock. "If you're serious, you can do the sweaters and other outer clothes. They'll go to the thrift shop here at the home. I guess underwear gets trashed, so that box is for junk to throw away."

Jane walked over to the boxes next to the bed. Sweaters were stuffed into one, the underwear was mixed with pens and scraps of paper in another, and the other boxes were still empty. She dumped three sweaters onto the bed and started. There was Susan's navy-blue lamb's wool cardigan that their bridge group had bought for her seventieth birthday. It had been the only present she had received and had brought tears to her eyes. Jane found tears in her own eyes as she smoothed the ribbing. She would be first in line at the thrift shop in the morning to claim that sweater.

Clarence cleared his throat. "Did you know her well?"

Jane carefully put the cardigan into the box and reached for a pullover. "As well as anyone here. She was a very private person." She paused but decided to pursue it. "Did you know her?"

"Yes."

Jane was glad her back was turned so he couldn't see the surprise she knew was in her face. She had thought he was from a social agency, called in by the Home. "Did...do you know her family?"

"Yes."

Probably worked for them, Jane concluded to herself. She had finished with the sweaters and turned around. "Anything else?"

"If you're sure you have the time, I haven't gotten to what's hanging in the closet."

Jane laughed aloud. "Time? That's about all I do have, however much I've got left."

At that, Clarence paused with a picture frame in his hand. He stared at her. She automatically smoothed her white hair, noticing all the brown spots and wrinkles on her hand as she did so. She smiled, then turned and walked toward the closet.

"It's hard getting old." He said it as a statement, not a question.

"Yes." She had to continue. "Especially without any family around you."

She sensed the stillness and turned back to him, a blouse in hand. He was staring at the photograph in the picture he held. She shuffled over to his side. The portrait sitting was of a smiling couple in their early twenties, probably taken in the 1940's by the woman's hairstyle. She looked vaguely familiar.

"Susan?"

Clarence nodded. "And Allen. In happier days."

"May I?" Jane reached out for the picture.

He nodded and handed it to her. "It seems to be the only one she saved."

Jane stared at the couple. Susan had rarely talked about her life before coming to the Home, only some allusions to a husband, and not very kind ones at that.

"May I?" Clarence held out his hand.

Jane nodded. "Where does that go?"

Clarence put it into a small box at his feet, one that held very little. "To the family."

"Oh." Jane folded the blouse. "Does this go in with the sweaters?"

Clarence nodded. "The coats can stay on the hangers. Mrs. McGrudder said she'll come by later for whatever is left."

Jane started on another blouse. "So what's the big mystery about this family? Are they in the witness protection program or something?"

Clarence's hearty rumble gave way to a somber face. "No mystery. So she never talked about her children? Or grandhildren?"

Jane tried unsuccessfully to hide her shock. Everyone else shared innumerable photos of cute little kids doing cute little things that only grandparents and great-grandparents can appreciate. Everyone but Susan.

"No surprise," continued Clarence. "She hasn't talked to them either for, oh, at least twenty years."

Jane laughed nervously. "That's hard to believe." She pretended to be absorbed in folding a knit dress.

"You liked her, didn't you?"

"What wasn't to like? Of course, it can get pretty lonely here if you don't join in the activities." Jane hesitated. "Susan was quiet and sometimes reluctant to socialize, but she always came around after I coerced her. She even seemed to enjoy our company."

Clarence nodded. "Good. As miserable as she was to her family, I'd hate to think she had a miserable life."

Jane arranged the dress in the box and turned to face him directly, arms crossed and lips arranged in a frown. "Okay, are you going to level with me now that I've saved you from the wrinkle curse?"

He nodded. "Mom taught me never to speak ill of the dead, but...." He frowned in concentration. "Trying to be kind, now, I have to say that she was extremely disappointed in her children and, after his death, in her husband. In retaliation, she pretended they didn't exist."

"All parents want their children to be successful, don't they?"

"Yes, but they also want them to follow a script. Become doctors or lawyers, find a nice girl or man, and produce well-behaved grandchildren." He shook his head. "Well, Harry and Mary didn't follow the script."

Jane was quiet during the pause.

Clarence picked up the photo of young Susan and Allen. "Harry decided he preferred men, openly joining a gay community in Provincetown. And Mary fell in love with the wrong man. Susan never forgave either of them."

"Yes, my generation tends to be rather quick to judge."

The big man nodded. "Allen was more open to his children's wishes, but didn't dare to openly oppose his wife. He sneaked them gifts and cards, even visited his daughter when the first grandchild was born. His ultimate betrayal, in Susan's eyes, was to include his children in his will, along with Susan. That relegated him to the mists of forgotten men in her eyes."

"But how could she...?"

A Fleeting Glimpse

Clarence grimaced. "God alone knows why people do some of the things they do. Even with all of that, I'm glad she had a friend here."

"Why?" It slipped out before Jane could think about it. "What does it have to do with you?"

"I was the wrong man, the one Mary married." He looked directly into Jane's eyes, challenging her to express her opinion. "Would you like to see pictures of our children, Susan's grandchildren?"

Jane hesitated only briefly. Then she smiled through her tears. "I'd love to."

K. E. Swope

Natural Talent

Benny rolled up the air hose. Then he rubbed his left hand, a touch of arthritis. He and Pauli had been going nonstop since early morning. All three modified race cars were ready for today's class of racing wannabes. Their boss, Rick Borden, crawled out of one.

Pauli poked Benny in the ribs and whispered, "Lookit. Ol' Rick soon won't be able to squeeze his jelly belly through that lil window. Wonder what he'll do then, huh? Maybe get a saw and make the hole bigger."

Benny chuckled and turned to toss the hose over the pit road wall. In his prime, Rick had raced one of these modifieds and won a few races. Now he held classes to let people try their hand at steering three-hundred horsepower engines around a half-mile track. Benny had been his crew chief for the past ten years. During that time, Rick had never won a race, although he finished in the top ten half a dozen times. Sponsors got harder to find. They wanted drivers who could take their product's name to victory lane. Even running in front was an asset, and youthful potential was even better. Those had been the glory days. Now Benny and the other hangers-on looked forward to these drive days to earn some extra money.

Rick came over to Benny. "Did you check the belts on number twelve?"

"Yeah, you were right about slippage. I tightened it so it should hold up for today. Might want to think about replacements."

Rick grunted. "Yeah, might want to replace the cars while I'm at it. That takes money, something in short supply. Just keep the damn things running. With today's fees, I've got enough to enter the season opener in two weeks. Maybe some sponsor will be impressed then and we can compete for another season."

"Sure thing, Rick." Benny grinned, adding to himself, as much chance of that as you dropping ten pounds. He'd never say it aloud, he wanted to keep going, too.

Pauli nudged him so hard that Benny nearly fell over. He pushed back, a quick jab. "Don't do that, Pauli. My ankle's still sore from when you dropped the jack too quick and the car landed on my foot."

"Sorry, but lookit that babe over there." Pauli pointed a sausage-shaped finger towards the grandstand fence, where today's customers were coming through the open gate in the fence.

A tall blonde walked next to a squat man dressed in sporty clothes. He was obviously dressed down in polo shirt, khaki slacks, and docksiders. Her casual navy slacks and waist-length jacket couldn't hide her curves.

"Wow," said Benny.

Pauli nudged him, more gently. "Wonder if he'll impress her enough with his driving today to get her...."

"Keep your mind on business," Benny interrupted. "No leering at the guests, Rick says."

"Yeah, but he's always flirting with the women," grumbled Pauli.

"That's 'cause he's the boss."

More people came streaming into the infield, gathering in small clumps until Rick called them together. He told those planning to drive to check in with his assistant, who would also collect any money still owed. Then he welcomed the group, sixteen people, drivers and guests. Pauli walked over to check Karen's list and came back to Benny with a smirk on his face.

"There's a bitch gonna drive today," said Pauli, ending with a chuckle. "Wonder if it's the blonde?"

Benny shrugged. "Don't matter. They're just customers, and we're to be polite."

Pauli snickered. "Oh, I can be real polite!"

Benny turned, too quickly. He winced at the pain in his ankle. Damn arthritis was setting in. He could dye his hair to look younger, but joint pains from all those fast tire changes were going to put him in a rocking chair before he was ready. Racing was a young man's game, like Pauli. Punks like Pauli didn't know how good it was to have a strong body that didn't creak when you moved.

"Pauli, you know, if you stay in this sport, one of these days, you might have to crew for a woman driver."

Pauli nearly choked. "No way."

"Way," replied Benny. "It's the wave of the future. They want equality in everything, and someday they'll get it. Even here."

Muttering and shaking his head, Pauli went to get out the racks of driver suits. Benny walked over to check with the ambulance driver and crew, wondering who had volunteered for duty today. He passed by the blonde woman and her companion.

"It just seems so dangerous, Mr. Parker," she said in a husky contralto.

"Now, Stef, remember today I'm 'Chet,'" said the man, his voice a condescending purr.

"Okay, Mr. Par….I mean Chet. Are you sure you want to do this?"

"Oh, it's safe enough or they wouldn't open it to the public."

"But there's a fire truck here. And an ambulance," said the blonde, with a real trace of worry in her voice.

"Just for show, Stef. All I have to do is put the car in gear and turn the wheel. A leisurely Sunday drive."

The man's smirk made Benny hurry on his way, shaking his head. Some people don't take it seriously, he thought. That fool will either hit the wall or be so scared that he'll crawl around the track. I'd better warn Rick.

Benny first chatted with the emergency crews to make sure they knew their responsibilities today. They had never had to make use of the safety volunteers, but there was always a chance. Rick had enough trouble getting insurance for his business. One requirement was to have both a fire truck and ambulance standing by.

By the time Benny finished going over the checklist with the emergency crews, he saw Rick starting the walk around. The drivers and any interested visitors, on foot, followed the path that the cars would follow around the track—low to the inside on the banked curves and far to the outside along the straight-aways, almost to the wall. The key word was 'almost.'

Shading his eyes from the late morning sun, Benny studied the group standing in the first turn. Even at a distance, Rick stood out, evident by his pear-shaped body. Benny wondered how many more years, and then stopped, resolving to enjoy whatever days he and Rick had left in the sport they both loved. Three women were in the group, the blonde and two others. One of them would be driving. When her turn came around, Benny resolved to find another chore for Pauli. His smart mouth while strapping in the drivers could be trouble, not to mention wandering hands.

Eventually the group returned. The members separated, some to put on flame-retardant coveralls and the others to find vantage points for photography. The blonde joined the group with the cameras. Benny admitted to feeling disappointed.

He studied the ten people searching through the racks of coveralls. Two older men with gray hair, half a dozen young bloods with dreams of a glamorous new career, one baby-faced male who didn't look old enough to drive, and a mature woman. Benny walked over to her.

"Can I help you, ma'am?"

She smiled, lighting up a plain face under gray hair. "You won't tease me, will you?"

Benny couldn't hold back a laugh. "No, ma'am, I certainly won't. I've been around this business long enough to know it's serious, not a teasing subject."

The woman sighed and said, "Thank you. I'm Minnie."

"I'm Benny, Rick's crew chief and assistant. That means I'm here to help him and everyone else have a safe and fun day."

The woman smiled again and held out her hand. "Pleased to meet you, Benny. And thank you for taking me seriously. My grandchildren think this is a joke." She pointed to the grandstand.

Benny saw a group of about twenty noisy people, mostly children. "Those all yours?"

Minnie shook her head, grinning. "Heavens, no. Only three, but they insisted on bringing all their friends."

"So you're doing it for them?"

Tears welled up in Minnie's eyes. "No, I'm doing it for my late husband. We met at a race track fifty years ago and went to races whenever we could. He always talked about trying it one day, but one day never came. And now he's gone, never got a chance. So I'm doing it for him."

Benny couldn't think of anything to say at first. Then he had an inspiration. "Well, then you seem to have an advantage over all the others. Your own guardian angel will look after you on the track."

A Fleeting Glimpse

A tear rolled down Minnie's cheek. She brushed it away and turned back to the rack.

When Rick climbed into his car to lead each of the other cars around the track, Benny walked over to start the drives. He called for the first driver on the list, one of the young cocks. Pauli knelt at the driver-side window to help him climb through, feet first, then fastened the five-point belt and slid the steering wheel on the column. Meanwhile, Benny motioned for the second driver, one of the older men.

At Pauli's signal that the first driver was ready, Rick gunned the motor in his race car and drove slowly down pit lane to enter the track. Pauli motioned for the guest driver to follow. The young punk gunned the motor and stalled the engine. Benny shook his head and watched Pauli's reaction. He was glad to see that Pauli was patiently talking the driver through the restart. Time to get the second driver ready.

Benny looked at the list and called for the second driver. "Don't let that young man's over-eager mistake scare you," Benny said to reassure the man.

The man grinned and said, "I won't. I've done this before and know how touchy the clutch can be."

Benny patted him on the back and sent him off to Pauli's care. Then he looked at the list and called out, "Chester Parker."

"Here," said the sporty figure who had brought the blonde. "Please, it's Chet."

Benny nodded. "Let's make sure your suit and helmet are a good fit. Then Pauli there will strap you in to keep you safe."

"This is quite an efficient arrangement with three cars," said Chet, nodding in approval. "Maximizing resources, minimizing time."

Benny stared at him.

"I mean, you don't waste any time, do you?"

"Oh, you mean alternating cars." Benny remembered his own advice to Pauli about being polite. "You've got a good eye. Yeah, we have to pay the track for our time, so we try not to have too much down time. We tried using three cars for the customers, but…."

"Too much investment in inventory," interrupted Chet, nodding again. "I can see that. While one driver is on the track for his ten laps, the next driver is being prepared in the other car. A third car wouldn't really speed things up, just add to the expenses."

Benny nodded and managed a smile. "Then when Rick brings one driver down pit road at the end of his laps, he keeps on going and the next driver follows him."

Two cars flashed by on the track, drowning out their voices. Rick led the way, and the second car followed, about three car lengths back.

After they passed, Chet asked, "How does Rick know how fast to go?"

"He watches his mirrors and slows if the following driver lags too far back."

Chet grinned. "Good idea here, but it wouldn't work in my business. I have to constantly push people to work a little faster. That young lady who came with me was really slow when she started, but now she's one of my hardest workers. I pushed her, you see."

Benny shook his head. "If we tried that, we'd have people hitting the wall. We gotta keep people safe, not push them past their comfort zone."

The double roar of two cars came down pit road. Rick continued slowly back onto the track, while the second novice started the engine. He didn't stall the engine, but moved out.

Benny waved Chet over to the pit wall. "As soon as that first driver is out of the car, Pauli will help you take his place. Any questions?"

Chet shook his head, watching the first driver climb out wearing a big grin. When Chet tried to enter the car head first, Pauli pulled him back and showed him how to go in feet first.

Benny felt someone standing by his shoulder. The tall blonde was taking a video of Chet. As soon as he was inside the car, she stopped and turned to Benny.

"Should I accidentally erase that very ungraceful entry?" Her voice was full of mischief.

"He your boss?"

She nodded.

"I think maybe a camera malfunction is a good excuse."

"I thought operator error myself"

Benny grinned. "But he thinks you're a good worker."

"At what I know," she said with a shrug. Then she smiled and put out her hand. "I'm Stefanie, but everyone calls me Stef."

"Benny here. You know how to operate that thing?"

"Not really, but I'm a quick study. As long as I capture the drive itself so he can show everyone at work on Monday, he'll probably forgive an early mistake. He bought this thing just for today and handed it to me when we got out of the car."

"Then he shouldn't gripe if it's not Hollywood style."

"Well, I'd better practice a bit. Later, Benny."

Benny turned to the next driver, the baby face. After checking the boy's suit and helmet, he sent him over to Pauli. According to the list, Minnie was next. Benny walked over to her.

"I see you found a suit to fit," he said to her. "How you doing?"

She smiled, lighting up her face. "Fine, really. I don't plan to set any speed records. My goals today are simple."

When she didn't continue, Benny asked, "What are they?"

"Don't laugh, please."

Benny crossed his heart and then his fingers.

Minnie laughed. "Okay, then, since you promise. First, I don't want to hit the wall. Second, I don't want to spin out. Third, I want to be able to hit all five gears in correct order."

"Those are great goals. I wish more of our customers felt that way. Most of them want to go as fast as they can. We try to slow them down to keep them safe."

Rick's car roared down pit road, followed by the second driver. Benny walked with Minnie to the car she would be driving. "Are you scared?" he asked.

She shrugged. "I have a healthy respect for that machine. I'll be fine."

"I know you will. Good luck, any way. And remember your guardian angel."

A sudden burst of engine roar interrupted them, followed by silence. Rick was already out on the track, and Chet had stalled the engine. Benny heard Pauli talking the driver through the restart, but it wasn't working. "'Scuse me," he said to Minnie. He called over the third helper to push the car while Chet tried to pop the clutch. After about twenty yards, the engine roared to life, stuttered, and then regained its rhythm. Bucking and jerking, the car slowly moved out onto the track.

Benny turned back to help Minnie into the other car, but Pauli was already strapping her in. The next driver needed to get checked out, but Benny took a moment to watch Chet's first lap. Ah, he's going to crawl, thought Benny. That's better than hitting the wall. He felt for the girl having to tape such a show, but it wasn't his problem. His job was to keep the show moving.

Benny needed to call the next driver. In the background, he heard the low frequency strain of a high-powered engine turning over too slowly. He hoped Chet wouldn't blow a cylinder that way. Rick would be really mad.

Finally, Chet followed Rick down pit road and stopped the car. Minnie was next, and Benny wanted to watch to see if she met her goals. First he called the next driver. Then Pauli called him over to help get Chet out of the car. The man's face was pale and clammy.

"Hurry, man," called Pauli. "Before he pukes all over the car."

Benny helped Pauli pull Chet out of the car as quickly as they safely could. The man couldn't stand up straight, just bent over pit wall. Benny hoped the girl, Stef, was being careful with what she taped. It wouldn't do her any good to show the other employees how their boss tossed his cookies at the track.

Benny asked, "Would you like some water, Chet?"

The man nodded.

"Come over here and sit down." Behind him, Benny motioned for Pauli to get the next driver in place. They had to keep the cars moving.

Chet sat down and took a deep breath. He finally spoke, in a cracked voice, "That's quite an experience."

"Yes, it is. People who've never done it have no idea of the danger." Benny knew how to play the game; Rick had taught them well.

"That's right." Chet sat up, noticeably straighter. "It really can be if one isn't careful not to go too fast."

Benny pointed to the track. "That woman knew the danger before she got into the car. She knows to be gentle on the gas pedal."

Chet nodded and managed a smile. Benny sensed someone standing behind him and turned around. It was Stef with the video camera.

She asked, "Are you okay, Chet?"

He smiled, a bit thinly but it was a smile. "What an experience."

"It looks scary."

Chet pulled his shoulders back. "It isn't that bad once you actually get started." He took another swallow of water. Then he looked up quickly. "Say, you ought to try it too, Stef."

The blonde took a quick step back. "Me?"

"Then we can both talk about it at work on Monday, compare notes, so to speak."

"I don't think so," she said, shaking her head. "Besides, you have to make reservations…."

Benny chimed in, "Oh, we're always ready to take an extra customer or two, if we have the track time."

"But I don't have that kind of money." Stef sounded very reluctant.

That reluctance seemed to fire up Chet. "I insist on paying. What about it, Benny? Is there extra time?"

Benny said, "Sure." Then he looked at the blonde, who was shaking her head and making strange faces at him. "Uh, anyway, I think there is. I gotta ask Rick."

Pauli came up to the group just then. "Ask Rick what?"

Chet spoke up. "Is there extra time to add an extra drive?"

Pauli looked shocked. "You wanna go again?"

"No, no, no. I wondered if my friend could have a turn."

Before Pauli could say anything, Benny pushed him toward pit road. "You have another driver to get ready. I'll take care of the paperwork."

Chet signed a check and Stef signed her waiver. When Chet walked away to take off his coveralls, Benny added a name to the list.

He asked quietly, "Why didn't you want to do this? It's really not that frightening."

"I know," said the woman. "I'll get a firesuit."

Rick was pleased to have an extra four hundred bucks, and Benny sent Pauli to check the final air pressure on the car tires. When the tenth driver left, Benny helped Stef to strap in. Only she didn't need any help. She slid in through the driver window like an eel slipping through a net. Before he could reach for any straps, she had them locked in place and tightened. With one click, she fastened the steering wheel and grinned up at Benny.

"I raced go-carts with my brothers for years," she explained. "I'm not frightened."

When it was her turn, Benny watched as she started up the engine smoothly and screamed out onto the track, nearly catching up to and passing Rick in the second turn. Her lap speed was less than thirty seconds, over seventy miles an hour, by the second lap. By the fifth lap, Rick had picked up the pace to keep ahead of this novice.

Benny looked around for Chet. Would he be taping the drive? Benny snorted. Of course not, Chet couldn't take a chance on a woman showing him up, especially not in front of his employees.

A Fleeting Glimpse

Happily Ever After

Constance Maguire sat in semi-darkness, curled up in one corner of her living room sofa. One table lamp was lit, since Greg had always insisted it be turned on as a deterrent to burglars. Outside the double doors across the room, Greg himself lay spread-eagled on the patio. She wondered if he was dead yet.

Taking another sip of merlot, she automatically looked at her wrist to check the time. However, her watch was upstairs on the night stand, along with the romance novel she had been reading. Now she sat alone, wondering what to do. Dawn would force her to make a decision, and she had no idea how long before the sun came up. Her soothing drink had no discernible effect on her inner turmoil.

Her stomach had been churning for hours, even before Greg went sailing off the balcony. Besides eating too much rich food, she had also been drinking heavily. She had tried to shut off her thoughts with alcohol. As a result, she could remember little about the evening after the dinner party. Vaguely she remembered the open door onto the minuscule balcony outside their bedroom and the thud on the patio below.

Connie shivered, although the patio doors were closed and the room was warm, even for early May. What a hellish week it had been, ever since Greg came home with news about his promotion, something he had been working for since the vice president had announced plans to retire. The promotion itself was the good news. The bad news was the rest of what he had said.

"It means I have to relocate to the West Coast," Greg had said last Friday evening, while they were dressing to go to the country club for their monthly dinner with his coworkers.

Connie had paused, her arms upraised as she checked in her mirror for darker roots in her blonde hair. "You mean, we have to sell the house and move?"

Greg cleared his throat, then continued tying his bow tie. "I suppose you could keep the house, if we can manage the finances."

She laughed. "That's silly if we're moving."

Greg paused before replying. "Uh, we're not moving. I am."

"You know long distance commuting can be the pits. Look what it did to Stu and Lisa." She walked across the room to give him a hug from behind. "Of course, we'll move. Oh, I know I'll miss my friends, but I can always make new ones."

"You don't understand," said Greg softly, turning around and grasping her hands in his larger, stronger ones. "I don't want you to come with me."

Connie stood silent and confused, staring into those gray eyes that had reflected her own passion for twenty-three years. Twenty-three good years of marriage, she had thought. "You're right, I don't understand."

Greg pulled his hands back and brushed his thick hair with one. He sighed. "It's just that I don't feel the same way about you anymore. I think it's time we both got on with our lives, but separately. The timing seems perfect."

"A separation?"

"Actually, a divorce. I'm planning to file the papers when I come back. I have to fly out tomorrow for a week to check the setup in the office and assess the situation. J.B. wants my proposal for any changes by a week from Monday, so I have to get moving on this. Perkins is just waiting for me to drop the ball so he can move in and claim the position is better suited to him."

"Oh." Connie's mind was spinning but her mouth was unable to frame a question. Instead she unzipped her dress.

"What are you doing?" asked Greg.

"Getting undressed. I don't usually wear a party dress to sit at home."

"We're not going to sit at home. We're having dinner at the club, remember?"

Connie stared at him, open-mouthed.

"Well, we can hardly call at the last minute and cancel. What would people think?"

Connie closed her mouth. "Yes, what will people think about us. 'Here come the Maguires, the ones who are divorcing, but they still have the nerve to appear in public together.'"

"Look, these people have been our friends. We can't stand them up." He avoided her gaze. "Besides, we don't have to tell them anything yet. In fact, I'd prefer not to until I have this job sewed up. I don't want to give Perkins any ammunition to undermine me."

"Well, at least I'm not the last to know," Connie said, her voice breaking.

Greg crossed the room and put his arms on her shoulders. "Look, I'm sorry this is happening, but I just don't love you anymore. And it's not fair to keep you in a loveless relationship when you have so much of your life ahead of you." He chucked her under her chin. "Come on, buck up, and look pretty. Consider this our own private celebration of being civilized about the whole thing."

The evening was civilized, with Connie more subdued than usual and Greg more congenial.

During dessert, Dee Perkins leaned over to Connie and whispered, "Are you okay?"

Connie nodded and picked up her coffee cup to avoid answering.

Dee patted her hand. "You look pale. There's a late flu bug going around. Maybe you're coming down with it."

"Maybe," replied Connie, wanting to confide in someone but worried about jeopardizing her husband's advancement in the company. She knew she and Greg could eventually work out whatever was bothering him.

On Saturday, Greg took a cab to the airport without saying much, except a reminder to confirm the menu with the caterer for their dinner party the following weekend. After he left, Connie wandered around the house, going from room to room, searching for the happiness that suddenly was missing. She picked up her latest romance novel, trying to immerse herself in the story. But her attention kept wandering back to the question of "Why?" What had she done wrong?

She thought she had done everything right. She had taken gourmet cooking lessons so she could impress clients Greg brought home from work. She had volunteered for all the social action groups so that the Maguires would become known as civic-minded individuals. She had developed friends among the wives because their husbands were the ones who could advance Greg's career. She had even agreed with Greg's decision not to have children until he could afford to take time away from his job to be with his family.

At that thought, the tears began, unbidden. The children she never had, the ones she dreamed about and longed for—and now probably would never have. By Sunday, she had cried so much that her nasal passages were clogged and she could hardly breathe.

On Monday she canceled her weekly bridge lesson at the club. She also called the wives auxiliary president for the police union to beg off from the charity luncheon, citing the flu that Dee suggested. Twice she dialed Dee's number, only to hang up after two rings. She tried to think of a way to talk about the situation, but gave up trying. After all, she just knew she and Greg could work it out and couldn't start gossip going when they got through this temporary glitch in their relationship. When her own telephone rang, she put a pillow over her ears to cut off its ringing.

On Tuesday, she applied extra makeup to put some color in her cheeks. After backing out of her weekly tennis lesson, she went shopping instead. At the bank, she was surprised by the low balance in their joint account, but found out the bulk of the money had been transferred to a separate savings account. Then she became worried but didn't know who to talk to.

Wednesday was the garden club meeting. Connie decided that she needed to get back into the world if she was to survive. However, halfway through the meeting someone suggested the group hold a fund-raising dance to honor everyone's wedding anniversary, and Connie left before she burst into tears. Again that afternoon she ignored her telephone.

By Thursday, Connie still had no idea what she could do to change Greg's mind but was determined to try. She called the caterer to confirm the menu for Friday's dinner and kept her weekly hair appointment. Having her hair washed and set, being fussed over, always made her feel better. It helped—a little.

A Fleeting Glimpse

The cleaning lady came and went on Friday morning as usual, and the florist delivered three arrangements to be placed strategically around the dining room. She tried on her new dress, pleased with the effect of the frothy peach frills that complemented her ivory coloring. Of course Greg hadn't really meant what he said. Maybe he had just been tired. Maybe....

The front door slammed, interrupting her reverie. Patting her hair, Connie walked down the stairs, then nearly tripped over Greg's bags in the front hallway. Greg himself was pouring a large glass of Scotch from the decanter in the dining room cabinet. His tie was askew and he needed a shave.

Connie cleared her throat. "How was your trip?"

Greg swallowed a gulp of liquor, then coughed before answering. "Fine. Everything's on track. That red-eye's a terrible way to fly." He looked more closely at her. "New dress?"

Connie turned around slowly. "Yes. Do you like it?"

Greg shrugged and took another swig of scotch. "It's okay. We have to keep an eye on expenses before we talk to the lawyer. I figured we could both use old Shapiro, since we can do this in a friendly fashion."

"This?"

"This...this...," Greg emptied the glass and plunked it down on the cabinet. "Hasn't it gotten through your thick skull yet that I want a divorce?"

"I thought maybe...."

"Maybe what? That I'd change my mind? Not a chance." Greg glanced at his wristwatch. "What time's the shindig begin?"

"Seven," replied Connie automatically. "Are we going to tell everyone tonight? Can't we wait?"

"Wait for what?" Then he relented and smiled. "Look, I know this isn't easy, but I'll tell you what, we won't say anything to our friends until we see a lawyer and start making some plans. Okay?"

Connie shrugged.

"I've got to get cleaned up. Why don't you check the liquor supply? I think we're low on gin, and you know Stu likes his martinis."

If asked, the guests would have agreed that the last dinner party given by the Maguires was perfect in every detail. Connie was more quiet than usual, but Greg made up for it by teasing the men and flirting with the women, all the while he made sure glasses were kept filled, especially his own.

After dessert was finished, the women moved to the living room, leaving the men to talk business while they dissected other women who were absent. Connie was only half listening, her mind in a turmoil.

"I heard Lily Jameson got a breast implant because her husband was losing interest."

"Someone told me Sue Olsten got an STD from her husband, but he blames her."

"I heard there's going to be a shakeup at the company, big changes."

"Yeah, people making lateral moves."

"You mean demotions."

Light laughter brought Connie back to full attention. Were they laughing at her?

"And I heard J.B. wants to expand the San Francisco office, eventually moving the company headquarters there."

"No wonder Sally Montrose has been campaigning so hard to move there so she can become the office manager."

"Great, get that man-eater away from our husbands."

Laughter again. Connie felt a stone dragging down her stomach. She tried her best to take part in the rest of the conversation, but she was suddenly feeling less certain of saving her marriage. Had Sally gotten her hooks into Greg? Nothing else claimed her attention.

Soon after that the men joined them to reclaim their wives and begin the exodus.

It was past midnight when the last guests departed. The caterer cleaned up the kitchen and tidied up the rest of the downstairs. Greg seemed dedicated to killing the bottle of scotch, so Connie went to bed. She decided he was past being lucid enough to make sense in a serious conversation. She had to try talking to him in the morning.

That was the last certain memory she had from the night before.

On the sofa, Connie now tried to take a sip from an empty glass. She was suddenly aware that she could see the design on the crystal clearly. Through the patio doors, pale blue sky was giving way to a yellowish blur on the horizon. She jumped up and stared outside. The pajama-clad body still lay on the flagstones. Try as she might, she could not remember pushing him. She also could not remember not pushing him.

Vaguely watching his body as it thrust open her bedroom door with a bang. Trying to evade his long arms, the reek of alcohol breath. Side-stepping as he made a lunge for her. Watching him trip on the carpet and fly head first flight out the door to the balcony and beyond. The thud, a hollow sound, with air being forced out of the body.

Worst of all, his low moans.

Now Connie walked over to the double door. She had to find out if he still breathed. And she had to decide what to do if he did.

K. E. Swope

The Day the Sky Fell

On that late afternoon in mid-June, May Belle Gardner knelt on the grass, carefully examining her rose bushes for aphids or other pests. She fought a constant battle against danger to her babies.

"You're looking very perky today, sir," she said, picking a stray leaf that had fallen since that morning.

Paul McCartney had no answer. He never did. Nor did any of the others named for real people, although sometimes robust Condessa de Sastago seemed to return May Belle's greeting with a nod of a glorious orange-red blossom.

Someone else answered instead.

A voice from behind her said, "Glad you think so."

"I wasn't talking to you, Glenn Prescott," called out May Belle.

She got up stiffly, using a nearby bench for leverage. She turned to face her neighbor, that upstart who thought he knew how to grow prize-winning roses. He was leaning on the wooden rail fence separating their yards, his gray hair barely showing from under the Australian bush hat he usually wore outdoors. He chuckled.

"You know, once you start talking to yourself, people may think you're losing touch with reality."

"Hmmph," she snapped back and began walking toward her back door. "The reality is that I know more about raising prize roses than you do. I always beat you at the flower shows."

Glenn grinned. "So you suggest I start talking to my rose bushes, too?"

"Course not."

As she opened the screen door, she heard his parting shot.

"Do they ever talk back?"

She froze, her teeth clenched tightly. If only she could think fast enough to come up with a snappy comeback to put him in his place. Then she relaxed her jaw and smiled. Her victory was at the flower shows, when her roses won first place in their categories, sometimes even the Gold Award for best in show. Meanwhile, he, her nemesis, could claim no better than second.

After checking herself for ticks or other hitchhikers, she stretched. Her arthritis was making it harder to kneel down. So far the pain hadn't kept her from tending to her roses daily, both in early morning and late in the day.

While the kettle came to a boil, she scanned her wall of honor. Several red ribbons from early attempts were scattered among a sea of blue. Mr. Lincoln had won three awards for most fragrant, and Margo Koster had garnered another one the year before. In her yard, they spread out along the edges of her flower bed so she could enjoy them without mixing their scents.

When the kettle whistled, May Belle brewed herself a special treat, Earl Grey tea with a dollop of honey. Then she settled onto the glider on her screened-in back porch with her latest mystery book. It was her favorite spot for reading because she could look out over her friends, the roses.

She hadn't realized she had dozed off until she heard a 'whoosh,' followed by a loud thump. Then a red glow filled her whole field of vision.

"Fire!" She dropped her book and jumped up. The whole sky was red.

She gasped. From the look of it, the whole neighborhood must be ablaze.

She tried to think what she should do. She picked up the teacup, then set it down again. She stooped over to pick up the novel she had dropped and set it down next to the teacup.

I wonder if anyone called the fire company yet. How could it have spread so fast? Why didn't I notice it before?

A veteran of many school fire drills, she decided panic wouldn't help. She took a better look at the fire—and laughed self-consciously.

A Fleeting Glimpse

This time she saw it wasn't fire. She should have known, she hadn't smelled smoke. All she really smelled was a whiff of gas. It wasn't the sky that was red. From where she stood at her screen door, she saw some sort of red fabric obscuring the whole sky and half her garden. It draped down like a circus tent to the rose bed around the birdbath.

"Oh, my goodness! What is it?"

She opened the door and stood on the top step. Overhead the red fabric covered her porch roof, falling away on both sides to enclose her backyard in a pocket of warm air.

Curious, May Belle walked over to touch the fabric. It felt like nylon.

The air was decidedly getting warmer, almost stifling. She felt she couldn't breathe.

May Belle grabbed the nylon with both hands and pulled. Maybe she could get it off the house and let in some fresh air. A gentle tug didn't make any difference, so she pulled harder, bending her knees and putting her full weight of nearly a hundred pounds into the effort. She was rewarded by the sound of a loud rip above her head and a rush of fresher, cooler air. She could even see a bit of blue sky through a slit in the fabric.

A man's voice called from somewhere outside her enclosure, "Stop pulling! You'll ruin it!"

May Belle let go of the nylon, which fell over her like a dust cover draping over unused furniture. She was being smothered. Before she could scream, the fabric miraculously lifted itself over her head. There stood a man with an armful of red nylon. He was frowning as he stared at the fabric still caught on the roof.

"Now you've done it," he snarled, turning to May Belle with a face nearly as red as the nylon. "You've ripped it good. Now I can't get her back up." He looked up at the house roof.

May Belle stared at the stranger, her mouth open. She adjusted her glasses to get a better view. He was tall and lanky, his long brown hair tied back in a ponytail with a piece of string that looked suspiciously like a shoelace. He wore denim jeans and a vest over a red plaid shirt. Carefully, he was tugging at the nylon fabric covering her roof, trying to dislodge it.

May Belle cleared her throat. "Excuse me, young man, but who are you? And what are you doing in my backyard with that...that...what is it?"

The man continued to tug the material from various angles. But the red nylon was firmly snagged.

May Belle tried again. "Look here, I think you owe me an explanation. And an apology would be nice for upsetting me so."

"Upsetting!" He turned and glared at her. "I'll say it's upsetting! Your birdbath's stuck in my gondola like a shish kebob. And look at that hole you've put in my balloon! It's going to be damn difficult to repair, even if I can get it loose without ripping it any more."

"Balloon? This is a balloon?"

"Lady, ain't you never heard of hot-air balloons?" Then he dropped the mound of nylon at her feet and spoke more calmly. "Sorry, lady, I didn't mean to come on so strong. It's just, I got a lotta dough tied up in this balloon. I'm trying to start my own business giving people rides in hot-air balloons. Oh, my name's Ike Somes. I've got a business card somewhere." He patted his pockets.

"You mean people pay you to take them up in a...a balloon? Is it safe?"

Handing her a smudged piece of cardboard printed with the words 'The Sky's the Limit Balloon Rides,' Ike laughed, a quick bark without humor. "For your first question, I hope they will. I'm just getting started. And second, I thought it was safe. Usually early morning and late afternoon are best, less turbulence. I guess I musta got caught in a down draft. Now, how'm I gonna get it loose? Ya got a ladder?"

A man's voice called out, "I rang the fire department for help." Glenn Prescott was hanging over the wooden fence between the yards. He aimed a camera at them and said, "Smile."

May Belle sighed. "I'm sure that wasn't necessary, Mr. Prescott. Mr. Somes, here, has everything under control. Don't you, young man?"

The young man scratched his head. "I dunno. Buck shoulda been here by now with the chase car. He musta took a wrong turn. At least I can pack most of the loose stuff in the basket."

"Basket?" May Belle looked around. "It must be a mighty big basket."

"You know, the gondola, the part that hangs underneath to carry people. It's over there."

May Belle looked over and saw something the size of a small car, made of heavy woven reeds, in the middle of her rose bed.

She shrieked and went running. "Oh, no! You've killed Paul McCartney!"

Ike's mouth dropped open. He turned to the neighbor. "She crazy or what? What's a star like that doing in a dump like Quakertown?"

Glenn Prescott burst out laughing. He took another picture of May Belle's house with the red fabric hanging from one peak like a limp sail from a mast. "I guess I better save some shots until the fire trucks get here. No, sir, she isn't crazy, at least not that way. She's crazy about her roses, though."

"They're just flowers."

Glenn smiled. "You don't understand. She chose each one of those varieties very carefully and spends more time with her roses than some parents spend with their children."

"Yeah, just stick 'em in the ground and let 'em grow."

The gray-haired man pushed his bush hat back to display the full effect of his glare. "We do more than that."

"Oh, yeah?"

"Yes," responded Glenn, more sternly. "It takes a lot of time and love to raise prize-winning roses."

Ike spun around as a finger poked him sharply on his shoulder. May Belle stood there, glaring at him although her eyes showed a telltale shine from unshed tears.

She continued. "Anything worth doing well takes preparation. Do you just wake up in the morning and launch your balloon?"

"Heck, no. I gotta check…."

May Belle interrupted. "Exactly. You don't think I just go out to my garden on the day of a flower show and clip a few blossoms, do you?"

"Well, I never…."

"Of course I don't." May Belle was under full steam by now. Her face was red and she poked her finger in Ike's chest to emphasize every other word.

"I fertilize spring and fall. Every morning I trim off dead blossoms to encourage new growth. And I have to snap off extra buds so that I get only one blossom on each stem. I take good care of my babies, and now they may not survive your attack."

Before Ike could reply, sirens announced the approach of fire trucks. Just before they arrived, a rusty gray pickup pulled up in front of May Belle's house. The long-haired driver jumped out and ran over to Ike.

"What the heck happened?"

May Belle answered first. "He landed his basket smack on top of my garden, that's what happened."

"No, I didn't land it there," said Ike. Then he turned to the newcomer. "Where you been, Buck?"

"Lost in a housing development that had no straight roads, only curves and lots of dead ends. So, downdraft, huh?"

"Yeah. Nothing I could do."

Neighbors had started gathering in Mr. Prescott's yard and May Belle's front yard while Glenn kept taking pictures. Two fire trucks arrived, and at least half a dozen firemen began running around, assessing the situation. Soon the head fireman consulted with the two owners of the balloon about the best way to get it off the roof without doing more damage to the fabric. Meanwhile, four others lifted the gondola off the birdbath, exposing the flattened greenery around it.

May Belle shouted, "No!"

Then she raced toward the devastation. The marble birdbath was intact, but the rose bed was a disaster. She knelt to examine each stalk, each leaf, each bud. All the bushes were flattened, nearly level to the ground, as if pressed between the pages of a book. Weeping, May Belle propped up stalks with pieces of broken stakes, oblivious to the crowd behind her.

Only when Ike tapped her on the shoulder did she realize it was getting late.

"Look, I hope there isn't much damage." He held out both hands to help her stand up.

May Belle ignored his offer and struggled to her feet. She said nothing in reply, just turned and stomped into her house.

It was nearly dark by the time the last spectator left and May Belle locked her doors for the night. She was so upset she forgot about her mystery novel.

She had barely finished her morning chores the next day before the craziness began again. The morning edition of The Free Press had a short description of the incident. Soon the phone rang for the first time.

"Ms. Gardner? This is Dan Crowley at Biggers and Stern. How are you this morning?"

"Fine."

A Fleeting Glimpse

"Are you sure? You had quite a scare yesterday, didn't you?"

"I suppose so."

"I'll bet you did. Have you called your doctor yet?"

"My doctor? Whatever for?"

The voice on the other end sounded worried. "You never know what kind of a strain such a shock can put on your heart."

May Belle was silent, not knowing what to say.

"Ms. Gardner? Are you there?"

"Yes, I'm here. And my heart is fine. But thank you for your concern."

"Well, it might seem fine now, but you never know what sort of residual effects such a strain can have at your age."

"Look, Dr. Crowley, I already have a doctor."

"Oh, I'm not a doctor. As I said, I'm with Biggers and Stern, the law firm on East Main Street. I'm calling to offer our services to sue the company that trespassed on your property. They caused damage, put your health at risk, maybe even your life."

May Belle was too surprised to speak.

"Ms. Gardner? Are you still there?"

"No," she replied, and hung up.

To the silenced instrument she added, "What nerve!"

She turned away but had taken only a few steps before the phone rang again. It was another lawyer. After she discovered the purpose of the call, May Belle politely but firmly thanked him for ringing. She hung up before he could say anything else.

The third call was from The Free Press, requesting an appointment to send over a reporter and a cameraman. May Belle referred the caller to Mr. Prescott, saying, "I'm sure my neighbor can provide you with all the pictures you want. He can also give you more details since he could see more than I could with that red canopy overhead."

Just as she hung up, the doorbell rang.

"Good morning, Ms. Gardner," said a young man with red hair and freckles. "May I present my card?"

May Belle automatically took it without looking at it. "Are you a lawyer or a reporter?"

"My name is Jim Dooley, and, yes, I'm a lawyer just getting started at Yarnell, Bartle, and Dischoff. I came to offer...."

"I'm not interested," said May Belle, shutting the door.

Then she locked it again before picking up the telephone to call Sarah Thompson, a friend and neighbor on the other side.

"Sarah, this is May Belle. I hope all the goings on didn't spill over to your yard yesterday."

"Not to worry," she replied cheerfully. "I've got a few footprints in my flower beds, but none of my plants were damaged. How did your roses survive?"

May Belle sighed. "I think I've lost Paul McCartney. And Cecile Brunner, too. I'm not sure about Mabel Morrison, but Margo Koster may survive. She's shorter than the others, so I hope the taller ones provided a buffer to give her breathing room."

"I'm sorry. I know how hard you've worked on your beauties. Can I do anything?"

"Not for the roses, thanks. The Free Press wanted to send out a full news crew. I sicced them on Glenn Prescott. Let them give the old goat some misery."

"Good for you. How are you feeling?"

"Funny, that's the same question all those lawyers keep asking me. I've had several offering their services to sue."

Sarah chuckled. "Not surprising. What're you going to do?"

"Nothing. And I mean nothing. I want to stay home and avoid talking to any more of those...those troublemakers. I wanted to let you know I'm not going to answer my phone or door until this dies down. Could you pick up a few things for me when you go out?"

So May Belle barricaded herself in her house with that pile of mystery novels to keep her company. Her only outside contact was the U.S. mail. She tended her roses early in the morning and late in the evening, when few people in the neighborhood were stirring.

As she expected, Margo Koster was reviving slowly, retaining a few leaves, although the shock of the impact would delay new growth. She wouldn't be back in full show-worthy shape in time for the flower show in two weeks. The other bushes, however, soon dropped all their leaves and showed no sign of recovery. Paul McCartney was in the worst shape of all. He had showed signs of being a grand champion in time, but those hopes were gone now.

A Fleeting Glimpse

May Belle tried not to read the newspaper articles about the balloon landing, but the photographs caught her attention. Someone had found an old picture of her with her rose bed. The layout editor had placed it next to her neighbor's picture of the mangled remnants—before and after. Glenn must have helped the editor with the list of rose varieties in the pictures. May Belle folded the paper and tucked it away in a desk drawer. Maybe she'd read it later, when the memory was less painful.

Then came a disturbing letter—a notice of intent to file suit by 'The Sky's the Limit' Ballooning Company. May Belle was so surprised that she nearly dropped the papers. A scrawled handwritten line from Ike Somes was at the bottom—"Sorry to do this, but it's the only way I can get any insurance money."

"Well, of all things," said May Belle, sitting down on the nearest chair. "Is he serious? I didn't make his balloon collapse. In fact, he crushed my roses."

That reminded her of all the lawyers. Maybe she needed one after all. A brief search turned up the business card from the young man with freckles. She called to make an appointment for the following week.

Over the next months, May Belle got to know Jim Dooley very well while the case went to court. He helped to present her side of the case, to gain the sympathy of the judge. In the courtroom, Ike Somes tried to get her to return his smile, but she couldn't understand why she should. He was the one who caused her all this trouble.

In the end, the two insurance companies worked out an agreement to satisfy the lawyers. May Belle's property insurance covered the cost of replacing her roses, and Ike's insurance company paid to repair his balloon.

One thing didn't end well—for the first time in ten years, since she had retired, May Belle had no entries in the county flower show. The next day, she tried not to look for the results in the paper, but she couldn't resist. As she had dreaded, Glenn Prescott won best floribunda and most fragrant. May Belle got some comfort that his roses did not win best in show.

The next morning, her doorbell rang. May Belle peeked out a window before opening her door. She wanted nothing to do with reporters seeking human interest stories that actually took no consideration for people's feelings. It wasn't a reporter but the delivery man from the local nursery, holding a rose cutting.

May Belle opened her door.

"Delivery for Ms. Gardner," said the man.

After he left, May Belle ripped open the accompanying card.

To her surprise, the rose was from Glenn Prescott.

"I want to win by beating you," was written neatly, "not by default. Here's a new Paul McCartney. Treat him kindly. We'll meet again next year."

Then she received a second disturbing letter. This one was just an inquiry, from the American Rose Society. They wanted to know where she had obtained her Paul McCartney. They stated it had been developed in Liverpool and not obtainable by U.S. growers until two months ago, but both newspaper pictures had shown a mature bush. The letter included a reminder that the U.S. Department of Agriculture strictly prohibited bringing plants into the country without submitting to the inspection procedures of the Plant Protection and Quarantine Offices. "Your prompt response would be appreciated," stated the closing paragraph.

May Belle couldn't believe it. When she had visited her nephew in England three years before, she admired his roses. Not intending to break any laws, she had brought back a cutting, wrapped carefully in plastic and secured in her suitcase, surrounded by dirty laundry.

"Oops," she said to herself.

As for the immigrant rose bush, a work crew from the Department of Agriculture spent two weeks with May Belle. They dug up all over the backyard but concentrated most of their efforts in the rose bed where Paul McCartney had resided. They sifted, and studied, and carried away plastic bags full of soil. Then they came back to check again. Under their thorough rooting around, all but Margo Koster succumbed.

May Belle tried to be polite. They were only doing their job. She just wished they wouldn't look at her as if she were a criminal.

Finally they declared her yard clean. "No infestations of any insects or disease not indigenous to the region," said the formal notice. Two weeks later she received a bill from the U.S. Department of Agriculture for three hundred dollars.

May Belle paid it, although reluctantly. She was slowly replanting her rose garden, but she knew it would take time to restore it to its former glory.

When Ike Somes sent her an offer for a free balloon ride, she politely refused. She added a plea for him to detour around her property when he took people up for balloon rides.

K. E. Swope

Amos and the Deaconess

Amos was minding his own business, when something whacked him across his shoulders. It hit hard enough to knock him off his bicycle and onto the sidewalk. He was thankful to land on his left knee, the one full of arthritis, and not the other one, the plastic replacement. The doctor had told him it should last at least five years, which meant he'd be over sixty when he needed to undergo that operation and intensive therapy again. Now he had other worries, though.

A strident voice came at him, a voice that seemed to come from high above, in the heavens.

"Don't you have any manners? Sidewalks are for pedestrians. That means people on foot, walking, just in case you don't know the meaning of such big words."

Shrugging his shoulders to test for injury, Amos ignored his attacker. After he decided nothing was seriously wrong, he looked up and mumbled, "I didn't hurt no one."

Above him stood a tall, stern-faced woman, her tousled gray curls peeking out from under a red-and-white striped tassel cap. She scowled at him, the corners of her mouth turned down so far that they almost met her chin. From between her crossed arms dangled a bright green cane, the assault weapon, Amos assumed.

The woman snorted like a horse. "Not yet, perhaps. What if an elderly person doesn't hear you coming from behind and moves into your path? Most of us don't hear as well as we used to, and many of us can't react quickly."

"Didn't stop you," called a voice from the crowd that had gathered.

Another voice offered, "Call the cops. She assaulted you."

The woman finally took her gaze away from Amos and scowled at the people surrounding them. She raised her cane and shook it. "The law says bicycles belong on the roadway, not the walkway. It's written like holy scripture." She pointed at two teenagers hugging their skateboards tightly to their chests. "The same goes for other wheeled vehicles, too."

"Huh, can't see me pushing no baby carriage down the street," muttered a woman.

"Yeah, and what about your wagon?" called another. "It has wheels."

The woman raised her chin with dignity. "Sidewalks allow for wheeled carriers being pushed or pulled by pedestrians, those who are walking legally along their designated pathway."

By now, Amos had managed to stand up with the help of two middle-aged women from the crowd. Concerned about his bicycle, he began to check for any damage caused by his fall.

Sensing no further excitement, the crowd began to disperse. Even his assailant paid no more attention to Amos as she stalked away, pulling behind her American Flyer, its red paint overwhelmed by crispy layers of rust. The wheels squeaked and clattered, rims beating a staccato at each crack. Empty soda cans in precise array were lined up inside the wagon.

"And good riddance to you, too, Deaconess," said one of the women who had helped Amos to stand.

"What's her name?" he asked, not catching the word.

"Don't know her real name," said the woman. "Folks around here call her the Deaconess like those Baptist women who run things at their church. Guess it's because she always acts like someone died and made her god. Plus she sometimes scolds the winos drinking out of plain brown bags about the evils of alcohol."

After that, Amos watched for her red-and-white hat that looked like a warped candy cane. Whenever he saw it in the distance, he made sure he wasn't riding on the sidewalk. He had never encountered her before the Lions gave him the bicycle. It had no gears or hand brakes, but it had extended his range of movement far beyond the few blocks he used to walk around. It also gave him a chance to improve his life a bit.

A Fleeting Glimpse

When he was fifty, Amos had fallen off some scaffolding at his construction job, smashing his kneecap and fracturing his skull. Although doctors replaced his knee, they couldn't restructure enough to give him back his agility to climb up and down ladders quickly. He was classified disabled. The one benefit was that he qualified for subsidized housing and received regular payments from the government. Because he hadn't saved for a rainy day, he had to make do on a limited income. Sometimes he made a little extra by doing maintenance work for his neighbors in the projects, but they had no more extra money than Amos. He began looking for another way to supplement the disability checks.

Amos had tried flipping hamburgers or bagging groceries, but standing in one spot for too long caused too much pain in his leg. He decided to pick up empty cans and bottles instead and turn them in for their deposit. Although it was time consuming to gather enough to make it worthwhile redeeming them for a nickel apiece, he had nothing but time to spend.

Before he got the bicycle, Amos was limited in how much territory he could cover by foot, unless he was willing to spend money to ride the bus. With the bicycle, he could cover a larger area and also gather more empties on each trip by tying a black garbage bag on each side of the handlebars for balance. He figured he could cover fifteen miles a day, which he did unless the weather was too wet or too cold. He always took the same route—out the cul-de-sac of the housing project, left on Maple, right on Main, down U.S. Route One to the business district, and then around the park back to Maple. He avoided the Deaconess, although he saw her sometimes in the area between downtown and the park.

That was until roadwork closed U.S. Route One in town. To avoid a possible flat tire, Amos went south instead of north the first day. As a result, he arrived at the town's playing fields early in the morning instead of middle afternoon.

At the parking lot entrance, he stopped to stare. A tall woman in a red-and-white tassel cap was stirring around the contents of a trash barrel using a long stick. The Deaconess.

Amos debated turning around, but he decided there were enough barrels for both of them. Since she was near the basketball courts, he rode to the bleachers near the softball field. He tipped over the first barrel and began sorting the contents—cans and bottles with a deposit went into his garbage bags, and everything else went back in the barrel.

A voice behind him said, "Hey, Gimpy, those soda cans are mine!"

Startled, Amos dropped the bag and turned around. He hadn't heard the Deaconess approach. Staring at her red face, he said, "What?"

Her face got redder and she waved her cane in the air. "I've been coming here every morning for seven years. You have no right to take away my cans!"

Amos crossed his arms. "Is your name on them?"

A crafty look came into her eyes. "No, but I depend on them to eat. What's your excuse?"

"The same. Can't work because of this gimpy leg." Amos forced a smile.

She snorted, possibly a suppressed laugh.

He was determined not to antagonize her because of that cane. "I've been stopping here every afternoon and finding cans and bottles. That means you haven't been taking them all, anyway—even if you have been coming here every day like you said."

The Deaconess drew herself up to her full height and stared down along her nose at him. "I don't touch beer cans, nor bottles. Even empty, they're the devil's work. You should be ashamed to soil your fingers with the taint of evil." She waved her cane through the air, a swish to the side to emphasize each forceful word. Amos was forced to duck if he didn't want to get whacked.

He tried hard not to laugh; she seemed so self-righteous, deserving her nickname. "Look, there's a solution. I'll take the beer cans and bottles, and you can take the soda ones. It's what you've been doing all along anyway."

"Hummph!" The Deaconess stomped off, her head in the air.

"You're welcome," Amos called after her.

There was no reply, but he hadn't expected one.

Amos continued to visit the playing fields first thing every morning, usually arriving before the Deaconess. Tipping over each barrel, he sorted the empties—beer cans and bottles in his bag, trash back in the barrel, and soda cans lined up on the ground next to the barrels.

Once softball season started, Amos often filled both bags at the fields. On those days, he turned them in at the closest grocery store before heading for the rest of town. Some days he got five dollars from the playing fields alone. Overall, there were so many beer cans and bottles at the fields that he set aside the soda cans without regret.

One morning Amos found barrels overflowing with cans that had contained a non-alcoholic beer. Must have been a sponsor, he thought as he stuffed them in his bags as fast as he could. He was on his second bag when the Deaconess struck.

"Those are MINE!" She punctuated each word with her cane rapping his wrist.

"Ow!" Amos dropped the bag and rubbed his wrist. "What'd you do that for?"

The Deaconess picked up the bag and carried it over toward her wagon. "Those are not beer cans. We had an arrangement."

Amos grabbed the bag and began a tug of war. "They're sold in the liquor section, so they're mine. Besides, they do contain some alcohol."

Suddenly she let go of the bag to raise her cane. Amos lost his balance and landed on the trash still littering the ground from the barrel he'd been checking. The bag landed on top of him, spilling out cans all over him. Not all of them were empty. His pants became wet and smelly.

The Deaconess put her hand to her mouth. Amos couldn't tell whether she was horrified or trying not to laugh. He didn't think it was funny.

He tried diplomacy. "Look, there's more than enough to share. Besides, you can't fit them all in your wagon."

"So I'll make two trips."

"And I'll wait till you leave the first time and take the rest!" Amos raised his voice to match her volume.

The Deaconess paused as if gasping for breath. Then the crafty look came back to her eyes. "I'm going to scream and tell the police that you're harassing me. If you're gone by the time I count to twenty, I won't."

"You…you…you wouldn't dare," Amos sputtered.

She crossed her arms and grinned. "Watch me. The count is now at fifteen."

Amos clambered onto his bicycle, beside himself with rage. He had only a single bag to show for his efforts at the fields. He peddled furiously. He had never had trouble with the police. In fact, he took pride in his integrity. He never stooped to shoplifting or lifting wallets. He had even returned a lady's purse when it fell out of her grocery cart. Now the Deaconess was taking advantage of him. It wasn't fair, after he had saved the soda cans for her.

He stewed about the situation for the rest of the week. He told a few of his neighbors, who laughed at first but then told him he should get even with her. Amos thought and thought but couldn't figure out how he could do something to her without getting into trouble.

"Just scare her, man," said the teenager from the apartment next door. "No law against that."

Amos snorted. "She'll yell harassment anyway."

"Not if she can't see you."

"I don't think I should."

The teen shrugged his shoulders. "So you just let her push you around. What are you, a man or a wimp?"

Amos shook his head. "I don't know. Besides, I don't have any idea what to do."

The teenager smiled, showing a mouthful of yellowed teeth. From his pocket he pulled a handful of round objects about the size of a gumball. Each one had a two-inch piece of cord sticking out of it. "Cherry bombs, man."

"No," said Amos. "No bombs."

"They're just firecrackers, man. You know, they go bang and make her jump."

Amos set the stage carefully during the next several days. He soaked twine in gasoline and set aside half a dozen soda cans. He waited a week to strike so his last encounter with the Deaconess would be long past.

On the target day, Amos got up at sunrise. He cut the twine into six-foot lengths, tying one end of each piece to the end of one fuse. He made the opening in each can a bit wider to slide a cherry bomb into it. He was ready.

Amos left his bicycle about a block from the playing fields. He placed the specially prepared cans in a barrel near some bushes. The opposite ends of the twine went through a hole in the barrel's side, facing the bushes. From other barrels in the area he pulled more soda cans to pile on top. This one barrel was overflowing with cans, an appealing lure for the Deaconess. Then Amos hid in the bushes to wait.

Before long he heard the squeaking wheels of the American Flyer. Amos smiled, anticipating the scare she was about to receive. He waited until he heard her footsteps approaching the barrel before he lit the ends of twine.

The flame flickered, then caught and began following the prepared path. Amos clenched his fists, willing the flame to remain steady, not to go out. It passed through the hole in the barrel. Then nothing.

Amos groaned. It had failed. The Deaconess reached for the cans in the barrel. Suddenly they leaped up to meet her. The boom echoed in the barrel. The Deaconess screamed and jumped back. Her wagon was behind her. She fell over it and onto the ground.

In the bushes, Amos rubbed his hands together with glee. It was more than he expected. The only way it could have been better was with an audience. Shrugging, he decided his revenge was complete. He turned to leave.

Then he realized the Deaconess was still lying on the ground. He had expected yells, but the only sounds he heard were cars passing on the nearby street.

He felt terrible. Yes, he had wanted to scare her, but now he was afraid she was hurt. If he stayed around, he'd probably get in trouble. He should leave, but he couldn't if she was really hurt. Maybe she was playing possum, waiting for the trickster to come out before she started screaming. So he counted to fifty, figuring that was as much patience as she could exert.

Still no movement. Amos sighed and walked over toward the wagon. The Deaconess was sprawled on the ground, her left leg bent at an unnatural angle.

"Rats!" Amos stooped. "Hey, lady, are you okay?"

No response.

He reached out and felt for a pulse under her chin. Thank goodness, her heart was still beating. He hadn't killed her. He hurried out to the roadway to flag down a passing car. Before long, he heard sirens coming but left before the ambulance arrived.

For the rest of the day, Amos stayed home, waiting for a knock on the door. When the teenager came to ask how the trick worked, Amos shook his head and said he'd chickened out.

The next day, he checked the newspaper for information about an attack at the park. The only details in the local news provided the woman's name, Marie Desmond, and her age as seventy-five. Nothing indicated the police were investigating a crime. Amos hadn't realized the Deaconess was so old.

He went to the hospital, but he stopped at the door to her room. The sleeping woman on the bed with her leg elevated in a pulley contraption looked old. As an avenging angel she had always seemed so formidable, not someone who should be lying so still and white on a hospital bed. He was tempted to go over and shake her, to make her wake up and yell or something, but just then a nurse came into the room and chased him out.

Amos continued to collect cans, both alcoholic and not, but he carefully kept money from the soda cans separate. At the end of a week, he had nearly eighty dollars that he figured would have belonged to the Deaconess.

On Friday afternoon, he returned to the hospital. He found Marie Desmond watching television. Even without her tassel cap, she was clearly the Deaconess, as Amos could tell by the glare she leveled at him. Luckily for him there were no sticks around to whack him.

Gathering his courage, he walked over to the bed and held out the bills. "Here."

The Deaconess turned her head and blinked. "What?"

Amos coughed. "Since you can't, I've been picking up soda cans, too. This is yours."

He put the money on the tray table next to her.

The Deaconess stared at the pile of singles but didn't say anything.

Amos turned and walked out. As he passed through the doorway, he heard a voice behind him say, "Thanks."

Office Etiquette

Janice admired the brass nameplate on her desk at Intertech, Incorporated. It stated simply, "Janice Simonetti, Human Resources." To her, it meant so much more.

Between her inner office and the world sat two assistants to field telephone messages, open mail and type correspondence. Today the connecting door was closed tightly, a rare occurrence. She needed quiet time to prepare for the next interview. On the resume appeared a name from her past. Janice had to ask the right questions: illegal ones could bring on a lawsuit. Although other employees would provide input after interviewing the applicant, Janice already knew what her recommendation would be. All she could do was record answers to her questions and send the applicant on to the next interviewer. Somehow, though, she had to prevent this person from being hired. Oh yes, she had to be very careful.

Nearly twenty years ago, she had applied for that first office job. She remembered every excruciating detail of that first day at A&S Services, along with the rest of her time working there. At the initial interview, the personnel manager said Janice's lack of computer skills would be no problem—she would have the opportunity to learn on the job. Seeing the other four typists tapping confidently at computer keyboards, Janice hoped her typewriter mentality wouldn't be a hindrance. However, she made up her mind to try and accepted the job offer. Although it paid less than she really needed, she trusted that perseverance would bring raises. She started her first day with mixed emotions of anxiety and enthusiasm.

The personnel manager introduced Janice to the supervisor, Arlene Hardesty. In front of a filing cabinet stood a woman nearly six feet tall, who looked around when they entered. Janice automatically put out her hand but quickly drew it back when it was ignored. After the personnel manager left, Ms. Hardesty sat down behind an oversized desk without offering a seat to Janice.

"Welcome to A&S, Simonetti," the woman said brusquely. Although she seemed no older than the typists in the outer office, her voice left no doubt who was in control. "You've got one week of probation to prove you can become a productive member of my typing pool. I've assigned Ralston to help you get acclimated. By Friday, I expect you to carry your own weight. Our productivity is down, and management is pressuring us to meet some heavy deadlines."

Ms. Hardesty's eyes shifted their unblinking gaze beyond Janice. "Oh, there you are, Ralston. I expected you to take charge of our new worker as soon as she got here. Janice Simonetti, meet Stella Ralston. Let's get to work."

The brown-skinned woman in the doorway smiled and said, "Hi, Janice." There was more warmth in the fluid tones of those few syllables than in all of the other woman's speech.

By the morning coffee break, Janice realized that paying her while she learned new technology was actually desperation on the part of the company. Rapid turnover of typists constantly resulted from the personality and expectations of the typists' supervisor. In her management style, last names were unadorned in addressing co-workers.

That night, Janice lay awake worrying about keeping this job. Since Dan had left her with two boys in elementary school, his monthly payments barely covered the mortgage. She had to fill in the remainder of what had previously been Dan's salary. Thanks to neighbors willing to watch her sons after school, Janice figured her schedule would work out. In return she would baby-sit for their children in the evenings and weekends when needed. Her first hurdle was to survive the week of probation.

At work, Janice couldn't figure out how to repay Stella for her patient guidance. Stella explained the basic workings of a computer with a concrete example. "Imagine," she said, "that the computer has school buses running between its components, carrying information and picking up or dropping off data along the way." She also showed Janice how to use function keys to work faster and how to keep track of multiple floppy disks storing files.

Janice soon realized that Stella was working extra time for no pay in order to finish her own assigned typing quotas. When confronted, Stella laughed self-consciously. "Don't thank me, girl. I have a selfish motive. I know you're capable and want to succeed. That counts for a lot. I figure it's worth some free time at first so you can take the weight off me later."

On Friday, Janice didn't feel capable when Hardesty appeared with a sheaf of papers. "Here's the draft of a proposal. Suppose it needs to be typed and ten copies made for a meeting in one hour. Tell me how you'd proceed to meet the deadline with a credible product."

Janice took a deep breath before starting. "I'd get out a fresh disk and start a file, labeled initial draft. After typing the text double-spaced, I'd use the spell checker and insert page numbers. Of course, I'd be sure to save the text on the disk, saving modifications early and often. Then I'd print it out and make ten copies for distribution."

"Okay, do it." Hardesty thrust the papers at Janice. "I want ten copies on my desk in half an hour."

"But," Janice said, "I thought you said an hour."

"I said for a meeting in an hour. Review committees need time to look it over before the meeting." Hardesty looked pointedly at the clock on the wall. "Time's passing." She stalked back to her office but left the door open so she could watch.

Janice told herself, I can do this. The other four typists were methodically tapping away at their own keyboards, eyes averted. They had probably all gone through the same test.

Janice pulled out a disk from a box of blank ones—then dropped it. She fumbled while trying to insert the disk into the drive. She pictured her two boys at breakfast that morning, asking her if she could take them to the zoo this weekend. I can do this for them, Janice assured herself as she began typing.

With one minute to spare, Janice walked into Hardesty's office and handed over ten stapled copies.

"Drafts aren't stapled. We use paper clips for easier handling. I'll talk to you after lunch." With those few words, Hardesty waved Janice out of her office.

Janice couldn't swallow the first bite of her sandwich. The other typists congratulated her on finishing the task. Janice couldn't be sure of her success until Hardesty gave her verdict. This job was important to Janice, not only to support her boys but also to bolster her self-esteem in her first real job. Besides, the health insurance alone was worth being intimidated.

With liberal swallows of water, Janice finished her sandwich. When she returned to her station promptly at one o'clock, there was a lump in her stomach the size of a softball.

Janice later discovered that Friday afternoons were noisy either with relaxed chatter after the week's tasks were completed or from fingers playing pizzicato on the keyboards to meet deadlines. Today, five pairs of hands typed quickly, but Janice's eyes strayed to the supervisor's door. Hardesty was taking a lot of time to check her work. Could it really be that bad?

By afternoon break time, Janice could stand the tension no longer. Instead of joining the others at the coffee station, she tapped at Hardesty's door.

"Come."

Janice held the knob and took a deep breath before turning it. Hardesty was writing with her head down and didn't look up. Janice stood inside the doorway for a moment, gripping hands tightly behind her back. Finally she couldn't wait any longer. Her voice quavered as she said, "Ms. Hardesty, how did I do?"

Her supervisor looked up at the clock before frowning at Janice. "I don't know yet. The meeting's still going on."

Janice felt the blood drain from her face. She gripped her hands harder. "You mean, it was for real?"

Hardesty croaked what could have been a laugh. "Of course it's real. We don't waste time on useless exercises."

Janice walked back to her station on rubbery legs.

Stella entered the typing room just then. "Any word yet?"

Janice shook her head.

Patting her on the shoulder, Stella said, "That's actually good news. It means the managers are discussing the fine points of how to cut costs or rearrange priorities to win the contract. If your typing hadn't been up to snuff, you would have heard about it as soon as they read their copies. So I think you're in. Welcome to the rat race!"

With that, she enveloped Janice in a bear hug. Through unshed tears of relief, Janice saw smiles and thumbs up from the other three coworkers. She asked, "Is there always so much pressure?"

Amid groans from the others, Stella replied, "Old Hardass really pushes when deadlines close in. Those of us who survive deserve some credit but we have to give it to ourselves."

Janice asked, "If it's so bad, why does anyone stay?"

Stella shrugged. "Different reasons. Mainly because the hours are good and we get benefits. Me, I'm going to school at night to get a college degree. Soon as I get that piece of paper, I'm making like a bullet—out of here. The others are biding their time, too, till something better comes along. Although there's not much chance for promotion, old Hardass isn't too bad if you don't antagonize her. Do good work and on time, and you'll be fine."

Fifteen minutes before Janice was scheduled to leave for the day, Hardesty piled the ten copies on Janice's desk. "Congratulations on passing probation," the supervisor said with no enthusiasm. "This is now your project. Next proposal meeting's at two o'clock on Monday. The managers need copies of the revisions by noon." She turned around and went back to her office.

Janice sat stunned. She looked over at Stella for reassurance.

"Just let me close up my file and I'll be right there," said her mentor.

Stella explained the process. "First thing on Monday, you need to go through the copies to see what comments are marked on them. Mostly they should all have the same agreed-upon changes, but if any disagree, you need to figure out which to use."

"But I don't know how...."

"Don't worry, just use your best judgment." Stella eyed her critically. "How are your English skills? Can you put together proper sentences?"

"I did get A's in high school English, but that was almost ten years ago."

"It'll come back to you," Stella reassured her. "It's like riding a bicycle—once you know how, you don't forget. Some of the managers evidently never learned. They really appreciate it when we clean up their grammar."

"But I thought I was hired just to type."

Stella chuckled. "Yep, that's all you're required to do. Trust me, though—the more you can help them with their writing, the more valuable you'll be to the company. That's something old Hardass can't take away from us. We make her look great."

Gradually Janice developed self-confidence along with computer skills. She also learned how to navigate around Hardesty's personality, following Stella's example.

Until Stella forgot her own lessons. She was training one of the never-ending stream of new employees, a few years after Janice's arrival. While helping the latest trainee meet one of Hardesty's deadlines, Stella led her student to the only copier on their floor, just outside the door to the typing pool. One of the typists was copying a thick document during a moment when she had no high priority projects. Stella asked her to "please" allow them to interrupt because they had a deadline to meet.

Hardesty, overhearing as she passed by, snapped, "Don't bother with 'please.' Just do it. We don't have time to be polite."

Stella responded too quickly before thinking, "There's always time for common courtesy."

The whole typing area fell silent.

Hardesty stopped her hurried pace and turned around. "What did you say?"

Stella stood her ground calmly. "I said we have time for courtesy."

Hardesty's face flushed. "Are you being impertinent on purpose, or is this your real nature showing through?"

Stella held her chin up. "No disrespect intended. I just have a lighter style of...."

"Oh, you have a style, do you? Implying that I'm too heavy handed!" Hardesty's face was mottled with shades of crimson to maroon. "I refuse to put up with such insolence. You are...."

"I quit." Stella spoke quietly, turned, and walked to her computer.

Hardesty stomped into her office and slammed the door.

The new trainee burst into tears and fled to the restroom. The other typists gathered around Stella's desk. Questions tumbled over each other.

"Are you really leaving?"

"What will you do?"

"Where will you go?"

One question dominated. "What will we do without you?"

Stella sighed. "Look, it was inevitable. I may have lasted longer than others, but even I have a limit. You'd better get back to work—you don't want to add fuel to Hardass's temper. Besides, I want to pack up so I can clear out today. A clean break is best. We'll talk at lunch."

That wasn't to be. The president of the company called Stella into his office just before noon, and she didn't return to the lunchroom. Gloom prevailed.

"If we present a united front," began one.

"They'll just fire us all," finished another.

"Besides," added a third, "I need the insurance."

Everyone nodded. They ate in silence.

After lunch, Hardesty prowled around the typing area, looking over their shoulders and picking up papers to check on the work being done. Janice could almost feel the static electricity in the charged atmosphere. In such a mood, everyone was at risk of Hardesty's wrath.

Three years of hard work seemed to vaporize. Janice felt on probation again. If only she had the courage to support Stella by walking out, too. However, after yearly raises she was finally planning to buy a new car. She had her boys to take care of.

Stella came back in time for the afternoon break, just as Hardesty was called to the president's office.

"Is he going to let you stay?" asked a chorus of voices.

Stella shook her head and smiled sheepishly. "The old man took me out to lunch! Can you believe it? He took me to lunch. He's even offered to write me a glowing letter of recommendation. Go figure."

Janice asked the question the others also wanted to ask. "But why didn't he make you change your mind and stay?"

"Well, he told me he values me as an employee and appreciates the quality of my work. But he added that he can't give people in supervisory roles responsibility without allowing them authority to run their departments as they see fit. If he undermines that authority, the company couldn't function."

Janice asked, "If he values you so highly, why doesn't he get rid of old Hardass and move you into her job?"

"Yeah!" agreed the chorus.

Stella lowered her voice. "Because she's his wife's niece. Also, her father pumped in lots of money a couple of years ago when the company was floundering. Nope, I'm outta here."

"What will you do?" Janice wasn't the only one to ask.

"First I'm going to divide my work among you." Groans met that announcement. "Then I'm going to finish cleaning out my desk. And then I'm going home. Now, get back to your work before old Hardass comes back and fires everyone...please."

Tentative laughs accompanied them all to their workstations. Tapping of keyboards was the only sound that greeted Hardesty's return.

Janice stayed after the others left, to help Stella carry out boxes of her personal items.

"What will you do?"

"I don't know," Stella admitted. "I planned to move on eventually, but not just yet. I wanted to finish my computer science degree first so I'd qualify for a better-paying job. I've got only one more semester, so I'll probably go flip hamburgers to pay for the last few classes."

Janice stopped short. "You mean, you've been planning to leave us?"

"Hey, girl, remember? This job is a dead end. We're only here to pay the bills while we plan our next step up. What's your next step?"

Janice suddenly realized she didn't have one. She hadn't thought beyond completing the next project, meeting the next deadline. Despite Hardesty's mood swings, the hours were right and she was learning so much.

As they parted, Stella reminded her to keep in touch. "You're capable of more than being a rat in the maze at A&S. Start preparing your own escape."

That's how Janice started college. After seeing how Stella smoothed things for her coworkers under Hardesty's thumb, Janice decided she'd like to learn more about supervising. Besides, she was now the one who filled Stella's shoes and trained the new typists. She signed up for a psychology course, with the same apprehension she remembered from her first day on the job. However, the instructor was much more supportive and encouraging than Hardesty had ever been. Janice got an A.

During the next three years, Janice met Stella for lunch from time to time. Stella had completed her degree as planned and was working as a computer programmer for nearly twice the pay as at A&S. "You really should study computers," she urged Janice several times.

Janice had decided instead on industrial management, thriving on the theory of supervisory skills to maximize employee capabilities. She acted as the buffer between Hardesty and the typists, calling upon her new knowledge to keep peace—and employees.

Then came the call. Stella knew of a job in the personnel department at the company where she worked, Intertech. It was just typing and filing to start, but the company was growing and the department was expanding.

Janice protested. "Why should I switch jobs? I know my job and my way around."

"Hardesty still your boss?"

"I'm managing okay."

"Doing her job at your pay, right?"

"Well, yeah." Janice grinned.

"You don't think she's going to get promoted so you can step into her job, do you?"

Janice laughed aloud. "Fat chance!"

Stella chewed and swallowed a mouthful. "Do you really want to keep doing that same job forever? Making Hardesty look good? Don't you think you deserve something better?"

Janice stopped grinning. "You have a point."

Stella was grinning now. "Here's the phone number of our human resource department."

It hadn't been easy to leave—Janice was respected for her good work. However, the increased pay had been the deciding factor. Furthermore, Intertech encouraged employees to continue their education by paying for college classes. People with ability and ambition were able to advance to better jobs.

In the following twelve years with Intertech, Janice had been promoted several times, until she reached her current position. Modular furniture intermingled with filing cabinets and computer equipment along the inner walls. Her desk and the tiered planter enjoyed morning sunshine streaming through the windows. She had come a long way since her first office cubicle. Six buds on the potted rose were nearly ready to burst open. Janice touched the warm soil, aware that she couldn't let the plants dry out, nor could she flood them. She had discovered the key to managing people was similar—finding the right balance between firmness and kindness rather than moisture levels. She was using the skills she had studied.

Now she picked up the resume on her desk, to brush up on the details. The head of the document production department was certainly justified in wanting this applicant interviewed. Over twenty years of management experience and glowing references. Available only because of the company being sold to a competitor, who was cutting back on middle level management.

Usually Janice felt secure in her decisions. She had worked in the personnel department for a dozen years before reaching the director's chair. This one interview would be a test of her abilities, much as that test at A&S nearly twenty years earlier.

She looked up at the framed certificate on the wall beside the door into her office. Although she couldn't read the words from her seat, they were burned into her mind: In deep appreciation for ten years of dedicated service. The signature was that of the founder and president at A&S. The testimony reminded her daily how she had conquered her trepidation at her first job. Remembering allowed her to treat job candidates with fairness. She had to keep that fairness in mind during the upcoming interview.

She reviewed the questions she had prepared so carefully, knowing she couldn't afford any mistakes. But, this was her job and she was good at it. She realized her stomach felt fine.

Her intercom buzzed.

"Yes?"

"Your ten-thirty is here."

"Thanks, Fern." Janice took a deep breath. "Send in Ms. Hardesty."

A Fleeting Glimpse

Promise Made, Promise Kept

When Adeline first met Jake, she didn't realize how fanatic he was about auto racing. He lived and breathed gasoline fumes and burning rubber. He took her to movies a few times, but then he showed his real side and asked her on a date to the local one-mile oval track.

That Saturday evening, she watched cars racing around to the sound of screeching and the smell of burning rubber. The cars, called Modifieds, didn't look at all like ones she saw every day driving the streets of her hometown. No headlights, no brake lights, no passenger seats, no doors, and the only windows with glass were the windshields. Jake explained that they were a smaller version of the ones that raced at the famous Indianapolis 500, but these had only about 300 horsepower in the engines. Their low-slung bodies still seemed to fly, skimming along only about six inches above the concrete.

Adeline wasn't too sure about Jake's passion, but she realized that if she wanted this man in her life, she had to accept his love of fast cars. Rather than stay at home alone, she started going with him to the track every week. Saturday evenings were noisy and smelly, but she and Jake shared them.

After Adeline and Jake married, they went to the local racetrack on nearly every Saturday from spring to fall. For thirty years, they watched cars scream around the track. Jake never worked on the race cars himself, but he read all the stock car magazines and knew enough to keep their own car in good running order.

"One day, my girl," Jake used to say, "I'm going to drive one of them monsters myself. I'm gonna rocket around and show all those youngsters that gray hair doesn't slow you down. One day, I promise you, one day."

One day didn't come. A massive stroke robbed Jake of speech and most of his mobility. When Adeline found she couldn't care for him at home, she had to place him in a nursing facility. For a year, she visited him every day.

One day, she took along a documentary that focused on how famous race-car drivers started their careers at small local tracks. It was actually an advertisement about taking lessons from racing schools. One of those schools gave lessons at the local track. Jake's eyes lit up when he watched the video, and he eagerly motioned for paper. Straining, he printed two words on the sheet: "lessons you."

Adeline laughed when she saw it.

Jake got agitated and printed two more words: "for me."

So Adeline called the phone number to inquire about taking a lesson at the local track. The young lady who answered the phone asked her only three questions. "Can you drive a manual transmission? Do you have a valid drivers' license? Are you over eighteen years of age?"

Adeline replied, "Yes, yes, and definitely yes." She chuckled and asked a question of her own. "Is there an upper age limit?"

"No, ma'am, but you have to be agile enough to climb in the car window."

Adeline hesitated briefly. She thought she could climb in that window; she knew the method, having watched all those drivers do it over the years. And she knew how to shift gears, after driving a straight-stick ever since she learned to drive. It gave her more control in bad weather, made her feel safer. She wondered how safe she would she feel on the track.

Determined to do it for Jake, Adeline set up an appointment. She asked a friend at church to videotape her experience so that Jake could see she did it.

Once she made the commitment and paid the money, she couldn't back out. She had promised Jake.

When she pulled into the track, though, she nearly turned around and raced for home. In the infield sat an ambulance and a fire truck.

A Fleeting Glimpse

They always came to the track to be prepared in case of an accident during a race. And now they were here, just for lessons. She realized this adventure was real, and it was dangerous.

However, for her, it was too late to back out now. She had been noticed, and someone was waving at her. It was Mr. Foley from church, with his wife and two small sons. He called out to Adeline as she climbed out of her car the regular way—by opening the door. She had thought about practicing the climb in and out the car window, but she was afraid the neighbors would think she was crazy. Besides, these modified race cars were only about five inches above the ground, so it should be easier than trying it with her station wagon.

"We were afraid you might change your mind," said Mr. Foley. "My boys think it's pretty neat that you're doing this"

Adeline grinned at the little boys. "Pretty crazy, huh?"

They nodded, with their eyes wide.

Just then a young woman called out, "Time for everyone to sign in."

Adeline joined the crowd moving toward the registration table, set up next to an open trailer. A lot of people seemed to want to drive a race car or else there were a lot of spectators. She began to get a fluttering in her stomach. The agitation grew as she walked past the three cars sitting on pit road. From this close range, they looked much bigger than she expected.

"Would all those who have signed up to drive today please sign the roster. Also make sure you sign the waiver that releases the track from liability. Spectators also need to sign the waiver, for insurance purposes. We need to know who's here today."

Adeline watched closely as several young men and one gray-haired gentleman signed the roster. Were no other women going to drive today? Just then, a tall blonde, probably all of twenty years old, signed her name. Somewhat relieved, Adeline signed on the line below the blonde, whose name was Brenda according to the list..

"Hi, Brenda," Adeline said, "I'm glad to see I'm not the only female driving today."

Brenda grinned. "Yeah, me, too. My boyfriend dared me, and I never turn down a dare."

Adeline raised her eyebrows. "Never?"

"Well, hardly ever." Brenda giggled. "Have you ever tried this before?"

"No, I'm definitely a novice. Have you?"

Brenda nodded. "Yeah, but my boyfriend went a lot faster than I did, so I want to improve my time. You know, go faster than last time. We're a bit competitive, but driving can be fun. Try to relax."

"That's hard to do. I'm probably out of my league among all you young people."

Brenda grinned again. "Haven't you ever heard about old age and treachery winning out over youthful exuberance?"

Adeline couldn't help the belly laugh that erupted. It helped to relieve the tension that had been steadily building all morning.

The two women walked over to the race cars sitting placidly along pit road. Brenda pointed to the first car in line, a brilliant cherry red. "That's Ted's car. He's the instructor. The other two are for us students."

Adeline walked closer to the monster she had to tame. When sitting in the stands as a spectator, she hadn't realized the size of the modified race cars. The top of each thick tire reached almost to her waist. She rubbed the smooth surface and asked, "Don't these tires slide without any tread?"

Brenda grinned before replying. "Yeah, that's the whole idea, to go fast. Ridges in the tread would just grab onto the track surface and slow the cars down."

Adeline gulped.

As if sensing her distress, the younger woman added, "Don't worry, though. Ted won't let you go any faster than you can control with the accelerator and brake."

Sighing, Adeline poked her head in the side window. "Not much room in here, is it?"

"It's definitely cozy."

"Not even room for a passenger," commented Adeline, pointing to a big metal box occupying the space usually taken up by a second seat.

"Oh, that's the gas tank."

Adeline pulled her head out of the car so fast that she bumped it on the top of the window. She'd be driving in a car while sitting next to a potential bomb.

She felt a hand on her shoulder and looked up. The blonde smiled gently.

"Don't worry," she said. "Professional drivers do it all the time. The gas tank is strongly made so it's safe as long as it doesn't sustain a hard hit. Not much chance of that because you'll be alone on the track, except for the driving instructor."

Adeline didn't have time to think about it any longer, for just then a chunky man with salt-and-pepper hair called out to the group to assemble near the registration desk.

"Hi, I'm Ted, your instructor," he said. "Now that you've all signed in, we'll begin the day's activities. First, I'm going to walk you around the track, along the path the cars will follow. It's called the groove. When we come back, my assistant will call out the first three drivers, and they'll find driving suits and helmets in the trailer over there. Okay, let's go. Spectators are welcome to join us."

With that, he led the group out onto the macadam. Adeline was surprised at how tacky the surface felt. As they approached the first curve, she felt her balance become more precarious. She hadn't realized how steep the slant was in the corners, meeting the grass of the infield but sloped upward to the outer wall. At first it made her feel more secure, because a car would drift downward if there were any trouble. Then she realized that centrifugal force would probably throw a fast-moving car toward the wall instead. Somehow the track seemed really narrow there, not allowing for much leeway. The butterflies were busy in her stomach.

Hastily she caught up to the group following Ted. He was explaining the groove.

"Now all you need to do is follow my car around the track. I'll be driving along the same pathway we're walking. Just remember, you're not allowed to pass me."

Others in the group chuckled, but Adeline was getting nervous again. That groove he talked about was close to the grass on the corners, but it got uncomfortably close to the wall on the two straight stretches. It looked and sounded easy. Why couldn't there be a yellow line painted on the paving? She knew she could follow a yellow line.

Back at the registration table, Ted called out the order of the drivers. Adeline was third, just right. Not first, so she would have a chance to watch some other drivers. She was also relieved that she wasn't last, because she knew she'd be a bundle of nerves if she had to wait long. Ted's assistant directed the first three drivers to find driving suits and helmets to fit them.

She followed Brenda and a young man with his hair tied in a ponytail into the trailer. Inside were two boxes of helmets and a rack of one-piece coveralls. Just like real drivers wore. Well, for today she was a real driver. That meant the coveralls were made of Kevlar to keep the driver from getting burnt in case the car hit the wall and caught fire. Again Adeline saw that gas tank sitting in place of a passenger seat. She was suddenly very glad for that fire truck and those paramedics.

Brenda helped her to put on the coveralls and reminded her to use earplugs before putting on the helmet. "Those three hundred horses make a lot of noise inside the car."

Taking a deep breath, Adeline walked out of the trailer, to be faced with Mr. Foley's movie camera pointed at her.

"Wave," he called.

Adeline waved one hand and forced a grin. Jake wouldn't need to know how scared she really was.

Then the show began. Ted called out the first name and then donned his helmet. He put his feet in through the window of his red car and somehow squeezed his round body through the opening. The tall young man climbed into the second car in line, and an assistant helped to get him settled. As soon as all the straps were fastened, the assistant gave a thumbs up signal. Ted's car started up with a roar. Almost immediately the student started his car—and stalled the engine. A second try proved more successful. Ted pulled his car out onto the track, followed by the student.

As soon as those two cars were safely away, the assistant motioned to Brenda.

"Wish me luck," Brenda called over to Adeline.

"Good luck," Adeline yelled. She hoped there was some left over for her.

Then Adeline turned her attention to the two cars on the track. Try as she might, she couldn't imagine a yellow line on that paving. Ted's path around the oval varied from down near the grass on the four corners to up near the wall on the two long straight stretches. Adeline remembered what he had said when he led them around the track, but would she remember when she was actually driving? Well, Ted had said, "Follow my car." How hard could that be?

All too soon, Ted's car came roaring into pit road, followed closely by the student. While Ted waited, idling those three hundred horses, Brenda fired up the third car. Adeline waved, but Brenda had her eyes straight ahead as she released the clutch and roared out of pit road to follow the instructor.

"Mrs. Kreutzer, you're next," called out the assistant. He was standing by the now empty car the pony-tailed young man had been driving.

Adeline's stomach turned over. This was it, her last chance to chicken out. Then she thought of Jake, lying in his bed at the nursing home. She couldn't back out now.

Taking a deep breath and forcing a smile for Mr. Foley, who was documenting the whole thing, Adeline walked over to the monster waiting for her.

The assistant grinned at her. "Can you manage getting in?"

"I think so," Adeline replied. Carefully, she lifted her right leg onto the bottom of the window, moved her weight onto it, grabbed the roof of the car, and pulled her left leg up to join its mate. Sitting with her feet inside the car, she turned and waved at Mr. Foley and the camera. She called out, "This is for you, Jake." Then she lowered herself into the interior of the car.

The assistant stuffed a cushion behind Adeline, so she could reach both pedals. Then he buckled the seat belts—one from each side across her lap, one from above each shoulder, and the fifth coming up from between her legs to collect the others in a tech-savvy spider web of safety. Once her helmet was safely secured, Adeline was ready. Then she had to wait while Brenda completed her fifteen laps. Adeline wondered how her new friend was doing.

"Any questions?" asked the assistant.

Adeline wanted to say, "Will you take my place?" She couldn't, though: she had promised Jake.

Suddenly a roar passed on the right, Ted's car on pit road. It was time to start the engine. Adeline did, but she promptly stalled it. On the second attempt, the car responded to her coordinated hands and feet. She easily found first gear, then second, followed by third and fourth. She was moving.

She stared hard at Ted's red car, trying to imagine a tow bar pulling her car right behind it. Suddenly there was a turn ahead of her. She tried to rotate the steering wheel gently to the left, knowing that if she jerked it too quickly, the car would follow her motion and head for the outside wall. Then there was the second turn, followed by a blessed straight stretch. She pressed down softly on the accelerator to try to catch up to the leading red car. All too soon she saw turn three just ahead. Instead of braking hard, which she knew could cause her car to spin out of control, she let up on the accelerator. The engine slowed, sputtered, in danger of stalling. Adeline realized she had to find a combination of acceleration and braking to keep her car under control. Ted had slowed his pace to keep just ahead of her, much more slowly than he had done for the first two, but she refused to be hurried as she tested her skills against this speedy monster.

The second lap felt more comfortable. Adeline noticed that the track's pattern seemed to be a regular oval but the third turn was not the same as the first turn. Although each one came after a straight stretch, turn one was easier to maneuver into than turn three. That one surprised her on every lap with how quickly it appeared.

Finally her dry eyes reminded her that she hadn't blinked. The engine's eight cylinders were pounding away right in front of her, reverberating inside her head despite the earplugs. She felt every bump, wondering if the car had any shocks at all to cushion the driver. With only five inches of clearance under the car, she felt every irregularity in the pavement.

The grass whizzed by on her left in the corners, almost close enough for her to pick a dandelion if she dared reach out. On the straight stretches, she tried to ignore the walls, which came too close for comfort to the right side of the car, the side with the gas tank. Adeline said many silent prayers as she followed Ted, lap after lap.

She began to get bored after a while, probably after ten laps. She started counting them too late to recognize the last lap, number fifteen. Suddenly the red car in front of her was turning left onto pit road. Thankfully, she followed slowly and applied the brake pedal gently. After going around the track safely, she certainly didn't want to spin out on pit road at the end.

A Fleeting Glimpse

When her car was at a complete standstill, Ted's assistant reached in and hit the off switch for the engine. In the silence, Adeline's ears were ringing. Slowly she unbuckled the belts and took off the helmet. Ted's assistant gave her a thumb's up sign and helped her out of the car, head-first this time.

Adeline sat in the window frame, savoring a moment of glory. She waved at the crowd and smiled broadly for Mr. Foley's camera. "That was for you, Jake," she called.

After she climbed out, she felt wobbly, so was grateful for a steadying arm from Ted's assistant. He said, "You did great."

Mr. Foley came closer. He asked from behind the camera, "So how fast did you go?"

Adeline turned to Ted's assistant. "There was no speedometer. How did I do?"

The assistant consulted his sheet. "Well, we count how many seconds it takes to cover each lap, then calculate the miles per hour. Finally we average the fifteen laps." He looked up at Adeline. "Your average was just about fifty-five."

Adeline couldn't stop a grin. "That may not seem fast, but I'm happy. I met my goals. I didn't spin out, I didn't hit the wall, and I got every gear in turn."

After all the student drivers had completed their laps, Ted handed out certificates and congratulated all of them on a job well done. He also invited them to come back and try to better their lap speeds.

Adeline turned to Brenda and said, "I don't think so. Once was enough for me."

Brenda just smiled and gave the older woman a hug. "Maybe. I think you were very brave to even try it once. I wouldn't be surprised, though, if you came back. The smell of burning rubber and gasoline fumes can become addicting.

Laughing, Adeline turned to Mr. Foley. "Here," said Mr. Foley, handing her a video cassette. "Show this to Jake. Show him you really did it. Tell him we'll be waiting for him to drive a race car one of these days."

With tears in her eyes, Adeline thanked the Foley family for coming to lend her moral support. And to document her accomplishment. For now that it was all over, she did feel a sense of accomplishment. She hadn't disgraced herself by running away from the challenge, nor did she let the power in the car get away from her. She just hadn't gone very fast. Maybe she would try again, to go faster. Maybe not.

The next day Adeline took the cassette along on her visit to Jake. When she started to play it, she saw Jake's eyes widen. He looked at her with surprise.

"Yes, dear, I really did it," she said. "I did it for you. And as soon as you get better, you'll have your chance, too."

Jake's eyes lit up.

"And then we'll see who can go the fastest," Adeline said, clasping his hand.

Jake made a coughing sound and then tried again. It sounded like he said, "Me."

A Fleeting Glimpse

My First Body

When Daddy got drafted, he told me, "Tad, you got to be the man around here while I'm gone. Help your Ma, and don't give her no sass."

To Rex, he said, "As for you, stupid mutt, be a good dog. No chewing up stuff."

Rex just wagged his tail, grinning with his tongue hanging out cuz Daddy was scratching behind his ears. Rex knew the joy of having that spot scratched but not what the words meant.

I did, though. I knew things was gonna be different, that I had to help out. I wanted to make Daddy proud, and I tried. I really did.

For a while, I did okay. I helped Ma with the chickens, chopped wood, even got some money for helping Mrs. Barstow on weekends. Rex didn't do much different, except he slept on Daddy's work boots and growled if anyone came near.

Ma did okay, I guess, except she was quiet a lot. And she didn't listen to the radio all the time like she used to. It seemed like every time she turned it on, they'd be playing something about silver wings and being one of America's best. Then she'd turn it off real quick. One of the guys at school told me it was about the Green Berets who go off to kill or be killed, with advice to a wife to have the son follow in the same footsteps. I didn't understand why Ma didn't like that, cuz I wanted to be just like Daddy.

When school started, I got to go to high school. I wanted to make Daddy proud, so I tried to go to school every day and pay attention. It didn't always happen.

One Friday, I decided to skip cuz the music teacher had a special treat for the class. Usually, I liked music class, but that day, the whole ninth grade was going to see an opera. I never saw or heard opera, but I'd been on field trips before. Usually, I got wicked sick on long bus rides, and everybody got mad at me. In the car with Ma, she let me sit up front with the window open so the air could blow in my face. Otherwise, my stomach got to feel like a banjo player was picking strings inside, up and down, up and down. Well, on the school bus, only the teachers got to ride up front in the first seat, and we wasn't allowed to open the windows unless it was real hot outside. November just wasn't hot enough for that. So I decided to skip it and avoid all that trouble.

I grabbed the lunch Ma packed me, the usual baloney and peanut butter sandwiches, and raced out the door. On school days, Rex stayed under the porch. As soon as he saw that brown paper bag, he knew where I was going and that he couldn't go. That day, I stopped at the shed for my fishing pole. When Rex saw me come out of the shed with my pole, though, he came shooting out so quick he left a patch of fur caught on a hook usually holding one of Ma's flower pots. His tail started wagging and I had to shush him real quick so he wouldn't get so excited as to bark. I knew Ma was in the cellar with a ton of wash to do, but she'd come running out of the house quick enough if she heard that old hound bark.

We got out of there without Ma suspecting me of anything other than a normal school day. If she asked about the opera, well, I figured I'd worry about that later. The sun was shining and maybe there was still a fish or two willing to chase after a worm before going to sleep for the winter.

Rex did his usual thing, wandering half a mile for every yard that I covered. He always came back to check on me once in a while, to make sure I hadn't got lost. I was crossing Witches Meadow, when I realized I hadn't seen him for a while. I called him, but he didn't come.

"Fool dog," I said. I didn't worry, though, cuz he'd find me when he got hungry. He loved baloney when I brushed off the peanut butter.

It didn't take him that long after all. He showed up before I got to my favorite spot, where the Swayback Brook spilled into Willamette Lake.

Sometimes the roiling water made the fish dizzy so they got confused and bit at anything that came near.

"Find a rabbit, did you?" I talked to Rex all the time. Ma told me I should start to worry if he ever answered me back. She didn't know he told me stuff all the time, just not with words.

Like then. He grabbed hold of my flannel shirt-sleeve and started tugging.

"Let go, you stupid mutt. If you tear my shirt, Ma will tan both our hides."

Instead of letting go, Rex started to whine, that grumble he does when he wants my full attention.

"Okay, okay. I'll come with you."

He finally let go and started trotting back the way he came. Every once in a while he stopped to look over his shoulder, making sure I was coming. When we got to a spot on the trail that crossed the dirt road where cars towed their boats to the water, Rex stopped.

"So? What now?"

Rex put his nose down to one of the ruts and sniffed. Then he looked up at me and grumbled again.

"Okay, so you found a trail. Smart dog. Now can I go fishing?"

I turned away.

Rex barked sharply, his version of "No, stupid!"

"Okay, okay," I said. I knew he'd give me no peace till I did what he wanted. He'd scare off the fish, too, if he kept it up.

With his nose to the ground, Rex headed down the narrow lane toward the lake. Before I got too far, I saw something shiny laying in a rut. It was a stone but it gave back the sun like it was gold. I put it in my pocket to show the guys at school. By then, Rex had disappeared, but he was still barking loud enough to scare the chickens out of laying eggs for a whole week. I figured I better go see what he found. It was the only way to shut him up so I could get on with my fishing.

When I found him at the edge of the water, he was sitting on his haunches, tongue hanging out one side of his mouth. He looked mighty pleased with himself.

"So, what do you want to show me?"

Rex barked once and pointed his snout toward the lake. There, in the shallows next to the concrete ramp, was the body of Ol' man Atkins. I knew it was a body cuz it was face down, and it wasn't moving none. I knew it was Ol' man Atkins cuz he was the only man in town who wore both suspenders and a belt with his plaid shirt.

"Did you do that?" I asked.

Rex just shook his head, like he was shaking off water after swimming.

"Sorry."

I hunkered down to look closer. Ol' man Atkins wasn't too bright, but he was smart enough not to fall in. Besides, I could see a big red splotch on the back of his head, like maybe dried blood.

"Uh, oh, Rex, we've got a problem. Looks like it wasn't no accident."

My stomach did flip flops, like I was getting car sick. I swallowed twice.

I watched Perry Mason on TV all the time, so I knew enough not to touch anything. But I still had a problem. If I ran into town to tell the sheriff about the body, the truant officer would get me. I could wait till after school, but that meant the killer had a head start and would probably get away. That thought scared me—no murders happened in our town.

"Too bad you can't talk for real," I said to Rex. "Then you could report the body, and I could stay out of it."

Rex just stood there with his tongue hanging out and his tail wagging. I knew my duty. Besides, it would be worth the scolding to be here on the scene and watch the action. Maybe I could help in the investigation.

I put my fishing gear in some bushes at the side of the road and tucked my lunch in the branches of a nearby tree. When Rex saw that, he cocked his head as if to say, "You don't trust me."

"Come on, boy, we need to get some help."

With that, I started running back on the dirt road toward the paved highway from Millersburg to the next town over. When I got to the concrete, I stood there to catch my breath and tried to decide what to do next. Should I try running to town, at least two miles, or should I wait for a car? I didn't have to make up my mind cuz I heard the Beatles singing that new song about a yellow submarine before I even saw the car. It was one of those Buicks with the big fins, heading toward Millersburg. I ran out onto the road and waved my arms like crazy,

A Fleeting Glimpse

ready to jump out of the way if the driver didn't stop fast enough. Rex helped by barking.

The Buick stopped and a red-faced man stuck his head out the window to yell at me. Before he could do more than take a deep breath, I hollered, "Get the sheriff. There's a body in the lake."

"Yeah, kid," the man said with a snort. "Halloween was two weeks ago and it's too early for April fools."

"Really, mister. I wouldn't joke about nothing so serious."

"Ain't you Frank Jamison's boy?"

I nodded.

The man glared at me. "Okay, I'll bite. Show me."

He followed me on foot to the spot where I saw the body.

"Well, would ya lookee there," he exclaimed. "I guess you wasn't funning' me."

I had to force myself not to say, "told you so."

"Okay, let's go get the sheriff," he said slowly.

I shook my head. "I'd better stay and guard the crime scene. Don't want no contamination of the evidence."

He nodded and took off. I was proud of my quick thinking. If I went with him, the sheriff would send me to the truant officer, and he'd take me home to Ma for a tongue-lashing. Staying, I could start looking for clues and put off Ma's yelling at me.

Me and Rex walked slowly around, trying to walk in the grass at the side of the path. He seemed to know this was serious. He trotted by my side, his nose dropping to the dirt track from time to time. We started at the roadway and were nearly back to the body when he stopped and barked one sharp yip. Then he pointed his nose at a dark spot on the edge of a deep rut. It was darker than the rest of the dirt, with a reddish tint. Rex went on another couple steps and barked again. This time there were two drops. Before we reached the edge of the water, the spots had become a steady trail. I was sure it was blood, so I was careful not to step on it.

"Wow, Rex, good job! Maybe you could be a police dog."

It looked to me that someone had dragged Ol' man Atkins down the dirt road to the lake. That meant there could be footprints. That also meant my footprints probably erased any others.

Then I realized it was a good stretch to drag a body. And there should be furrows made by his heels dragging. Of course, it could be the killer was really strong and could carry him. No, I decided, Ol' man Atkins was too big for anyone except a circus strong man to carry that far.

"A car, Rex. There must have been a car."

It had to be a big one to get down that bumpy road. The county had dumped a load of stone last year and tried to smooth it out. Most of the fill got washed away by spring rains, but the ruts were still worse than a roller coaster.

That seemed the answer until I realized that the blood would be inside a car instead of leaking on the road. Maybe a pickup truck, with the body tossed in back. Lucky all the rain we had a few days before had packed down the dust, so maybe there'd be tire tracks in the dried mud.

Before I found any more clues, I heard the siren. Sheriff McIntyre was coming. I sat on the grass at the side of the dirt road and pulled Rex down to lie at my side.

The sheriff stopped several yards away. He was scowling as he walked over to me, careful to walk in the grass at the side.

"Well, Tad, what kind of trouble did you get yourself into?"

I smiled, even though that banjo player had started on my stomach. "Not me, Sheriff. I just found the body."

His scowl deepened. "This better not be one of those jokes you boys like to play."

"No, sir. I wouldn't joke about something like this. It's Ol' man Atkins."

The sheriff looked surprised. "Are you sure?'

"Lest somebody else you know doubles up his belt and suspenders."

"You stay right there," he ordered. He turned and stalked across the grass to the edge of the water.

I hugged Rex around the neck. We waited what seemed like hours until the sheriff returned. He didn't say nothing, just stalked past us and back to his car. He called on his police radio for a deputy and an ambulance. Then he turned and walked over to where me and Rex was sitting. Before saying anything, the sheriff sat down next to me and took off his hat. He wasn't scowling anymore.

"Okay, son, let's have it."

I told him about coming down the dirt road to go fishing and how Rex was the one who told me about trouble. After all, I had to give credit to the real hero. I also told him about the spots Rex found.

"Show me."

Telling Rex to stay, I walked on the grass to point out the trail of spots and then the start, where there was just one or two at a time.

"I figure there should be tire tread marks to track."

The sheriff looked at me strangely. "Is that so?"

When I explained my reasons, he nodded. "You interested in the law?"

I shrugged. "I watch Perry Mason, but I never thought there'd be anything like that here."

"No one would. Everyone around here liked Ol' Herb. Heck, he was always lending a hand where it's needed."

"Yeah, he fixed our water pump when a hose broke. And he helped Mrs. Barstow dig up for her garden cuz her husband's on the road so much."

We sat quiet for a while.

Without looking at me, he asked, "No school today?"

I swallowed. "Um, yeah, er, nope."

He looked at me. "Which is it?"

Taking a deep breath, I plunged in. "Well, there was a field trip to see an opera, and I always get sick on long bus rides, and everybody gets mad at me, and…"

"And you don't really like opera." He sounded kind. "I understand. But you still have to report to Mr. Graves when we get back? Right?"

I nodded without looking up. I got up to get my fishing pole and lunch. Before I took more than two steps up the road, the sheriff called to me.

"Where you going?"

"Home."

"No, you're not," said the sheriff. "You need to stay here so we can vouch for each other that we didn't tamper with evidence. Got it?"

I looked up. He actually had a grin on his face.

"Got it," I said. "What you want me to do?"

"Well, let's see. How about if you keep your dog over there, out of the way, so he doesn't mess up any evidence. You could eat your lunch while we wait."

So me and Rex sat under a tree and shared my sandwiches while the sheriff went to his car to write in a notebook.

Deputy Slocum showed up before I finished my lunch. Rex didn't pay him no mind, just wiggled the tip of his tail, cuz he was waiting for the bread crusts. Me and Rex ate the cookies while Sheriff McIntyre gave his deputy orders. Then he turned to me.

"Okay, Tad, let's go."

Drat, I wanted to watch the medics pull the body out of the water. Ah, maybe the gold stone was important. I pulled it out of my pocket.

"Could this be a clue? I found it in one of the ruts. Maybe the killer dropped it."

The sheriff grinned and shook his head.

"Sorry, son, it's just fool's gold."

"What's that?" I asked.

Rex grumbled. He wanted to know, too.

"Part of the load of stones the county spread," the sheriff explained. "If you look around, you'll probably find lots more."

"So it ain't worth nothing?"

"Afraid not. Just to you, remind you of today."

"Yeah, and all my detentions, probably till the end of the year."

I almost threw it away. Then I figured maybe Ma would like it and wouldn't get so mad at me.

The sheriff put his hand on my shoulder.

"I'll put in a good word for you with Mr. Graves."

"Ma, too?"

"That I've got no control over."

Nobody said nothing while we walked to the police car, not even Rex.

Sheriff McIntyre asked, "Want to sit up front?"

"Can I?"

"Sure, but Rex has to sit in back."

"Siren, too?"

A Fleeting Glimpse

The sheriff shook his head. He tossed a dog biscuit into the back of the car, so Rex was happy to jump in. He liked the windows being open, too.

When we got to my house, Ma came out with a sick look on her face.

The sheriff opened the car doors for me and Rex. That dumb hound ran to Ma, his tail wagging and a grin on his face. I was smarter cuz I knew I was in for it.

"It's okay, Mrs. Jamison," the sheriff said, walking over to Ma. "Tad isn't hurt."

Ma looked at me, still not smiling. "But he's in trouble, isn't he?"

"Well, yes and no. Can we go inside and talk?"

I sat on the floor with my arm over Rex, worrying about what Ma would do to me for skipping school. Sheriff McIntyre told Ma about what happened. She gasped and leaked a few tears when she heard about Ol' man Atkins. Sometimes she just gave me that look. I knew that look real good. Since Dad got drafted, she gave it to me a lot. I hated it and tried not to do stuff that brought it out. It was hard.

Finally the sheriff got up. "Tad, you showed good thinking today. Try not to miss any more school if you want to go into police work."

"What about Mr. Graves?"

Sheriff McIntyre looked at Ma before answering. "I'd say Tad isn't feeling very well today. What say, Mrs. Jamison?"

Ma didn't say much after he left, just looked at me with sad eyes while she cut up a chicken for supper. I hated when I disappointed her. When Dad left, he told me to be the man of the house, and all I did was make Ma sad.

After supper, I asked if I could do the dishes, but Ma shook her head.

"I think you need to go to your room and think about school. You need an education so you can do something with your life. Besides, you have to get up early to get to Mrs. Barstow's house."

The next morning, Ma smiled at me again. "I love you, you know."

I nodded, afraid I'd cry if I said anything.

"I packed your lunch, some leftover chicken. Be sure Rex doesn't get any of the bones."

After I put air in my bike tires, I rode a couple miles to Mrs. Barstow's house. Ma hated to use gas unless the weather was bad.

When I got there, Mrs. Barstow was already hanging out wash.

"Morning, Tad," she called. I thought that's what it was cuz she had a couple clothes pegs in her mouth.

"Morning. What's to do?"

I parked my bike next to the garage and put my lunch in the old refrigerator inside. There was root beer there for me, just like usual. Rex headed over to sniff her cars, the big Cadillac her husband loved and her little Corvair. He liked to find out where they'd been.

"The Caddy needs a good wash," she said, carrying the empty laundry basket to the back door. "Don't forget the tires."

"How about the Corvair?"

Washing her cars was my favorite job cuz she let me drive them in and out of the garage. That V-8 engine in the big car sounded neato when I put it in neutral and revved it up. I wanted to buy me a car like that someday.

Mrs. Barstow called out through the screen door, "Only if there's time before lunch. Concentrate on John's car. He'll be back tomorrow from a cross-country haul and expects his car to shine."

After I backed out the Caddy, Rex started sniffing at the back bumper. He started grumbling in his throat, telling me, "Look what I found."

I was busy filling a bucket of water at the well, so I didn't pay him no mind. When I walked over to the car, he barked at me so that I nearly spilled the water.

"Fool dog! Pumping that water ain't easy, so don't you make me spill it."

He barked again. Then he grabbed my hand and pulled me toward the car.

"Okay, okay, I get it. You want to show me something. So show me."

He grumbled again, let go my hand, and pushed his nose against one end of the bumper.

I stooped over. There on the top of the metal bar was a blob of brownish red. It looked like…could it be…dried blood? I stepped back real fast and tripped over the bucket. It spilled and I landed on my rear end.

"Rex, I think we got a problem."

He licked my face and whined. I scratched behind his ears, thinking. Mr. Barstow was on one of his long hauls, so he couldn't have done it.

A Fleeting Glimpse

What if Mrs. Barstow killed Ol' man Atkins, tied him to the bumper, and dumped him in the lake? Wow, that would be something.

"I don't think so, Rex. She's too nice to kill anybody. Besides, she's too tiny to carry such a big body all by herself."

Before I stood up, I saw something shiny underneath the bumper. It came from the tread on the rear tire. I crawled over to get a better look. Stuck in the tire was something that looked like gold. I pried it out with my pocket knife.

"Hey, Rex, it's more fool's gold."

Rex grumbled that he knew that.

"Uh, oh, that puts this car at the crime scene. Maybe. Whadda you think, Rex?"

Instead of answering, he decided to go chase a rabbit that came hopping out of the bushes. He was no help at all.

I washed and waxed the gleaming black metal, making the body shine real good. When I washed the bumper, I worked around the spot I thought was blood. I couldn't get rid of what might be evidence. I knew Ol' man Atkins helped a lot of people, but what did he do to get someone mad enough to kill him.

Rex and I shared the cold chicken, but I drank the root beer myself. Rex didn't like it cuz the bubbles tickled his nose. After lunch, I started raking leaves but I started feeling sick before I got many raked. I must have looked bad too, cuz Mrs. Barstow sent me home, telling me to take some bicarb.

Instead, I pedaled to the police station. I hoped Sheriff McIntyre would be there. A deputy told me the sheriff was off duty, so I was tempted to go home and forget about the car. He'd think it silly for little Mrs. Barstow to be our murderer.

Then I remembered that Perry Mason didn't ignore clues, even if they turned out to be false leads. So I looked that deputy in the eye and told him I had important information about a murder.

The deputy laughed. "Sure, kid."

"But I found the body yesterday."

He looked at me funny, but he picked up the phone. His fat fingers just fit in those little holes when he spun the dial. Soon the sheriff showed up, wearing jeans instead of a uniform and with grease under his fingernails.

"This better be important. I was working on my pickup."

"It's about a car," I said. "I think I found the one that took Mr. Atkins to the lake."

That got his attention. We went into his office, and he made me sit down. Rex followed and sat next to me. I held on to him while I told the sheriff about the spot on Mr. Barstow's Cadillac and the fool's gold in the tire.

Sheriff McIntyre laughed. "Those may be good clues, but I know John Barstow's been hauling steel to California, been gone near three weeks. And Herb Atkins was over at Widow Sitwell's two days ago to fix her roof."

"Oh," I said.

The sheriff stood and put his hand on my shoulder. "You did the right thing by telling me, and I'll check it out. Now you'd best be getting home before it's dark."

Ma made me dress up and go to church with her the next morning. Rex knew as soon as he saw me in my suit that he couldn't go. He didn't even grumble when Ma pulled our old Chevy out of the barn.

We got there just as the preacher was getting wound up. I was sure everybody knew about me finding Ol' man Atkins and was staring at me. I kept my head down the whole time. Ma pulled me out of there before the preacher said the last "Amen."

The phone rang as soon as we got in the door. Ma talked real quiet and looked at me a lot, but didn't say nothing to me. After that, she didn't answer the phone. I had my chores almost done when Sheriff McIntyre's police car pulled in our drive. Rex ran over and tried to jump in when the sheriff got out. I quick ran over and pulled him away.

"Your Ma home?"

"Yeah, in the kitchen."

I still had to put fresh straw in the chicken coop, and I knew I'd get an earful if I didn't finish. By the time I washed up and got to the kitchen, Ma and the sheriff was sitting at the table, drinking coffee like nothing unusual had happened.

"There's some root beer in the fridge," said Ma.

A Fleeting Glimpse

I wanted to sit with them, but I figured it was an adult conversation. When me and Rex headed upstairs, the sheriff cleared his throat.

"Tad, come sit down. You need to hear this," he said.

I looked at Ma, but she was staring at her empty cup, her face all red. I pulled out a chair next to her, and Rex sat close, nearly pushing me off. I took a swig of my soda, then looked at the sheriff.

"Thanks to your detective work, Tad, our murder has been solved."

I looked at Ma, but she wouldn't look at me. I didn't know what to say, so I didn't say nothing.

"It was Mrs. Barstow who put the body in the lake."

I shook my head. "But she's so tiny…"

"Desperate people do desperate things. It seems that Ol' Herb was visiting Mrs. Barstow…." He stopped and looked at me funny. "Then he just died."

Ma choked, so I pounded her on the back.

"Yeah?" I said.

"Well, according to Mrs. Barstow, he just collapsed and had no pulse. His heart must have given out. The autopsy should be done in a few days, so we'll know what killed him then. Given the circumstances, I'd say she's telling the truth."

"But how could tiny Mrs. Barstow move the body?"

The sheriff shrugged. "Sometimes desperate people can do the near impossible. She was out of her mind with worry about what would happen if Ol' Herb's body was found in her bedroom, that she dragged it outside on a plastic shower curtain. It was too heavy for her to lift into the car, so she decided to tie it to the bumper. I found the rope, extra clothesline in the garage under some old rags."

Rex butted his head against me. I was so rapt up in the sheriff's story that I forgot to pet him.

I asked, "Why not the Corvair?"

"Mrs. Barstow worried that it wouldn't be powerful enough to haul the load through those ruts going to the lake. Once Ol' Herb's head started bumping up and down, the skin broke open and leaked the blood."

Something was bothering me, something from Perry Mason. Then I remembered what I learned one night. "But," I said, "the heart stops pumping blood after it stops beating. How come there was blood afterwards?"

The sheriff looked surprised. "You really do pay attention when you want to, don't you?"

I just shrugged, but I looked him in the eye cuz I really wanted to know.

"Well, son, there's a lot of blood in the head, and when the Caddy drove over all those ruts, Ol' Herb's head was a bumping up and down, eventually opening up the skin and letting blood out. That's what you noticed." He paused, then continued. "Thanks to your keen eye, we found out we don't really have a murderer around here after all."

Ma finally looked up. "Tell him the other news," she said.

"Well, Mrs. Barstow says she won't need you to help her out any more on Saturdays."

"Oh," I said, then turned to Ma. "I'm sorry. I know you depend on that money to help out."

The sheriff cleared his throat. "I have a suggestion, Mrs. Jamison. We could use someone around the station to sweep up, maybe help with the filing if they prove trustworthy. What do you say, Tad? Think you could handle it?"

I nodded, afraid I'd choke up if I tried to talk. Maybe I could pretend to be Perry Mason.

Betrayal

Brenda sat at her kitchen table, a full mug of cooling tea at her elbow. Outside her bay window, timid January sunlight fought through thickening clouds. She stared at the open wedding album in front of her. Staring back at her were two young people, her much thinner self and Joe with a full head of hair. She pulled out that formal portrait and deliberately ripped it apart, top to bottom. Just the way Joe had ripped apart their marriage that began so happily nearly thirty years earlier.

Two years ago that same happiness had still existed. At least she thought it had, with a nice house, an attentive husband, and a college-educated son making his way up the corporate ladder at a computer company. Even if his wife hadn't been Brenda's idea of what was right for her son, Joe Junior seemed happy, and that was what was important. What more could any woman hope for?

Then Joe came home with an idea to celebrate their twenty-fifth wedding anniversary.

"How would you like to go to Hawaii?"

Brenda was almost speechless. They had wanted a honeymoon in that paradise but couldn't afford to travel all the way across the country, plus part of an ocean. Instead, they had spent a weekend at an inexpensive cabin on Cape Cod. Since then, Joe's swimming pool company had prospered.

Finally Brenda found words. "Can we afford it?"

Joe grinned. "You bet. I just signed a contract with the Pacquinta chain of hotels to install spas in the suites of all their New England hotels. I'd say we can afford a few trips."

Brenda hugged him. "I'll check out the travel section when I go to work tomorrow at the library."

Instead of answering, Joe handed her a stack of brochures. With a twinkle in his eye, he said, "I don't know how to choose, they all look so great." Pulling out one paper from the stack, he added, "But I thought maybe a cruise around several of the islands would be good for our first visit."

Brenda sank down on the sofa, placing all but one of the brochures on the end table. The one she held onto was advertising a cruise onboard the Norwegian Line's Pride of America. The four pages of pictures and descriptions painted a fairy-tale story of four of the major Hawaiian Islands. It would be so romantic, just the two of them in paradise.

Joe poured himself a beer and sat down next to her. His next words surprised her.

"How about we take Joe Junior and Gloria, too? For a belated honeymoon trip for all of us, a special one like we couldn't afford and they can't either."

He took a swig of the amber liquid before propping his feet on the coffee table. At a glance from Brenda, he quickly removed his shoes before returning his stocking feet to the glass top. Brenda smiled at him; he was learning to be civilized in the nice house she had arranged for them.

"Joe, I don't think they can afford to go. They have huge college loans, and any savings they have are going toward buying a house."

Joe studied the half empty glass in his hand. 'Well, I really made a sweet deal on this contract with Pacquinta, so I can cover a trip for four."

She considered how to react. Although she felt vaguely disappointed at him wanting to share this special trip with others, J.J. was their son. He and Gloria were family, not strangers. Perhaps on this trip she would learn to know and love her daughter-in-law better.

"Then I guess it's a lovely idea."

After initially protesting, the younger couple gracefully gave in to Joe Senior's enthusiasm. From Brenda's perspective, she saw Joe Junior protest. She overheard his wife of two years telling him how much fun it would be. When a date had been agreed upon, Joe Senior made the arrangements.

"All you two youngsters have to do is get the time off from your bosses."

Before they could leave, the women needed to do some shopping.

Joe convinced Brenda, "You can use some new fancy duds, my girl, and Gloria can help you choose them."

The two women spent several Saturday afternoons at the dress shops, looking for cocktail dresses and lounge wear. Brenda had to admit that Gloria had a good eye—she knew which colors and styles were just right for Brenda.

When Gloria looked longingly at a chartreuse ankle length dress in chiffon, Brenda entered into the excitement of the excursion. She could start breaking down the walls between them before they even began the trip.

"Try it on," she urged her daughter-in-law.

Gloria grimaced. "I can't. It doesn't fit our budget."

Brenda patted her shoulder. "Look, I don't need to buy five fancy dresses. Joe will gladly pay for them, but I can manage with four. We just won't mention the fifth one was for you."

"I have to tell J.J. He'll wonder where it came from."

Brenda smiled. "Tell him it's an early birthday present."

After a flurry of packing, the big day finally arrived. Joe arranged for a limo to drive them to the airport in New York, where he managed to upgrade their seats to first class.

"Joe, you're spoiling me," Brenda said, as they sipped champagne onboard.

"Nothing's too good for my girl," he replied, leaning over to give her a peck on the cheek.

Across the aisle, Joe Junior and Gloria were already absorbed in the travel brochures. Brenda heard them discussing all the possible excursions at different ports.

She heard her son whisper loudly, "Why can't we just stay onboard when the ship docks? "

"We can't come halfway around the world and just look at the shore from on the ship. There are so many interesting places to visit."

"Right, but all those tours cost extra. We don't have hundreds of dollars just to see a lava field. The documentary on public TV was really thorough." He was no longer speaking in a whisper.

Joe Senior leaned across Brenda to speak to the younger couple. "Hey, you two, just figure out which sights you want to see, and we'll manage. We have two days in Honolulu before the cruise starts. How about we each make a list and we'll compare notes at the hotel tomorrow morning at breakfast? That goes for you, too, my dear." The last was addressed to Brenda.

Over a late breakfast, the four of them compared notes. Everyone agreed on visiting the Arizona Memorial later that day, which wasn't far from their hotel.

Brenda wanted to visit the Polynesian Cultural Center the following day, and J.J. said he had some coding to do for a computer program due for delivery the week after their return.

Gloria frowned. "I want to go to Waikiki and do some snorkeling."

Joe Senior yawned deeply. "I think this old body would like a day to catch up to the clock."

Brenda felt her shoulders droop. Her husband must have noticed.

"But don't let me spoil your day, dear. You go see the hula dancers; I can book you into a tour bus leaving the hotel in the morning. We'll spend today on our serious pilgrimage to Pearl Harbor, and then each one relax tomorrow before we get caught up in our whirlwind vacation on the cruise. Once onboard the ship, we'll be spending plenty of time together."

That seemed to set a pattern for the rest of the trip. They ate meals together and spent evenings at the shows onboard, but the days varied. Sometimes all four of them toured together, such as visiting the lava field at Mauna Loa, but many days their interests diverged. Brenda preferred touring the coffee and pineapple plantations, J.J. avoided as many of the excursions that cost extra because his father insisted on paying, and Gloria was avid for anything daring, such as parasailing, hiking up a mountain to see the sunrise at an ungodly hour, and flying in a helicopter over a secluded valley. Joe Senior split his time between the two women and tried to press his son to join them on more tours, mostly unsuccessfully. J.J. thanked his parents for the trip, but explained that the timing was not the best for him because of the computer code he had to write and deliver in its final form a week after their return.

"Dad, I really need to do this perfectly. My job may depend on a finished product that has no bugs in it. Surely, you understand how important it is to get myself firmly established with this company?"

Joe Senior agreed, but Brenda heard Gloria complaining to J.J. about neglecting her. The trip was turning out to be less than a perfect honeymoon.

She was relieved when the trip ended. She had seen beautiful sights that she had only dreamed about before, but tension between the two young people was almost visible. How well she remembered those first few years of marriage when she and Joe had danced around each other, trying to find out how to fit comfortably in each other's lives.

The real world came back abruptly. Joe had nightly meetings with his planning staff to set up hiring schedules to meet the demands of the new contract. J.J. seemed to disappear into his computer lab, preparing for the final product delivery for his company. Brenda was called in for extra hours at the library because so many people were ill. She didn't hear from Gloria, which wasn't unusual, but she hoped the two young ones had made peace with each other.

A month after they returned home, Joe dropped the bomb.

"I want a divorce."

Brenda was standing at the sink and had to grab onto the edge to keep from falling over. "What?"

He repeated, "I want a divorce."

Brenda gulped and turned to face him. "Why?"

Joe looked at the floor instead of at her. "We've grown apart, old thing."

"But we can work this out. If I've done something…."

"It's not something you've done or didn't do," Joe said, interrupting her. "We just don't have anything in common now that J.J. is on his own."

Brenda couldn't believe what she was hearing. She had been the dutiful wife while Joe built up his business. The only reason she had started working part time was to keep the boredom at bay. She could play only so many games of bridge and volunteer for only so many charity events. All as 'Joe's wife,' to put forth the face of the supportive wife of the community leader he wanted to be.

"What can I do?" Brenda asked, trying not to whine. It was true that the thrill had long disappeared from their relationship, but she thought they had settled into the contentment of mature older people.

"Nothing," Joe said rather sadly. "I just need space."

"We could try a separation."

Joe shrugged. "That won't change the way things are. Look, I'll agree to any terms you want. You can have the house, the Mercedes, and whatever alimony we can agree on. I won't contest it. Let's not make a big deal over it. Be mature adults who've changed from those starry-eyed youngsters of a quarter of a century ago."

Brenda tried a few more times to convince Joe to try again, but without success. 'Irreconcilable differences' seemed an apt expression for their status.

J.J. didn't seem upset when she told him the news."

"Shit happens," he said.

Gloria did not comment.

With no contest, the divorce took less than two months to arrange. Brenda shook her head at that—it had taken three times as long to plan the wedding. The proceedings were civilized, although Brenda felt like throwing up each time she appeared in court. She had failed in her marriage.

Two weeks after the divorce was final, J.J. called her.

"Mom, sit down. I've got news."

At last, Brenda thought. She had been waiting for most of the two years of his marriage to hear those magic words, that she was going to be a grandmother. She could still salvage something out of her failed marriage, helping J.J. and Gloria raise their own children.

"Gloria and I have separated."

Brenda was glad she was sitting down. "We must have a bad connection. I don't think I heard you right."

"Mom, Gloria has left me."

"Well, you know the first five years are the hardest, honey. You have to learn how to put up with each other's idiosyncrasies. With counseling…."

"No! It's over. No counseling. No reconciliation."

"How do you know unless you try?"

Brenda heard a sigh at the other end. "But we'd both have to try. And Gloria isn't willing."

"Are you sure?"

Changing the subject, J.J. asked, "Have you talked to Dad lately?"

"Why, no, I haven't. After we signed the divorce papers, we shook hands and wished each other luck. I wanted to kick him in the behind, but I thought that would be inappropriate in the lawyer's office. We decided to try giving each other space before contacting each other. I'm hoping that he'll come to his senses after a while, instead of throwing away all those good years."

She heard a sigh at the other end.

"Mom, those good years have passed. He's not coming back to you."

Brenda felt herself smiling. Ah, the certainties of youth. "Your dad has good common sense, dear. He'll come around."

J.J. groaned. "I didn't want to tell you this yet. But I don't want you to hear it from someone else."

"Hear what?"

A pause. "Gloria has moved in with Dad."

Disputed Remains

The knock came at ten twenty. Julie Armstrong had just turned off the television and taken her Labrador retriever, Shadow, out for his final visit to the backyard. Her hand on the light switch jerked back when the first of three sharp raps sounded on the front door.

God, don't let it be Ray, she thought. Since their divorce two months earlier, he had made a habit of coming around at late hours to plead for her to take him back. When Julie filed a restraining order, he started phoning instead. Grabbing the portable phone, so she could dial the police if Ray had reverted to visiting, Julie went to her front door.

"Who is it?"

"Police. We need to talk with you."

Julie drew in a sharp breath. She had no outstanding parking tickets, and the kids were safely asleep upstairs. It had to be about Ray.

A woman's voice came through the door this time. "Please open the door, Mrs. Armstrong."

Julie did so. Two uniformed officers, a man and a woman, stood under her porch light.

"I guess I don't need to ask for identification when you're wearing those uniforms." Julie felt embarrassed by the quivering in her voice.

The man pulled out his badge. "I'm Sergeant Tobin and this is Officer Masters. May we come inside?"

Julie pulled open the door and stood back for them to enter. She gestured to seats in the living room. As usual, Shadow lay sprawled across the sofa. He opened one eye to inspect the newcomers, but his only other response to their presence was a wriggle at the tip of his tail.

"Off," Julie ordered. Then she shrugged. "He's old and thinks he runs the place."

"Don't disturb him on our account," said Officer Masters, patting the dog as she passed by to sit on one of two armchairs. Sergeant Tobin took the other, leaving Julie to choose between the piano bench and the sofa next to Shadow. She chose her dog, sensing she needed his comforting warmth. The police never brought good news.

Sergeant Tobin cleared his throat. "I'm afraid we have some bad news. Your husband has been in an accident."

"My ex," whispered Julie, all she could manage.

Sergeant Tobin looked confused. "You are Mrs. Armstrong, aren't you?"

Julie nodded. "But we're divorced."

"Identification in his wallet lists this as his address and you as the person to be notified in case of emergency."

Julie sighed. "He couldn't accept that it was over. I had to take out a restraining order to keep him from coming around, drunk, at all hours of the night."

"I see."

"Is he hurt? Did he hurt anyone else?" Julie had always feared Ray would take someone along on his journey to self-destruction. She said a silent prayer that he hadn't.

Officer Masters replied this time. "I'm sorry, but he didn't make it. His pickup went off an embankment and rolled over several times. He wasn't breathing when the paramedics reached him. But he died on the way to the hospital."

Julie was surprised to feel tears filling her eyes and threatening to spill over. She had thought Ray had killed off her feelings with his drinking.

The female officer reached out a tentative hand. "Will you be okay? Is there someone who you'd like to call to stay with you?"

Julie shook her head. "No." She cleared her throat to start again. "No, I made my decision to remove him from my life. Now I just have to decide how to tell our children, Emily and Jason."

Sergeant Tobin asked, "Who else needs to be notified? Parents, brothers, sisters?"

"Just Frankie. That's his son from a first marriage."

"Do you have his address?"

Julie shook her head again. "He moved out soon after...well, about two years ago. I heard he got married last year, but...." Her voice faded. How to explain the angry words between son and father?

Officer Masters stood up. "Are you certain you can manage? We can send around a social worker tomorrow."

Julie patted Shadow's head. "This is my social worker now."

Sergeant Tobin also stood up. "Will you be available to come by tomorrow to identify the body?"

Julie stiffened. "The body?"

"Yes, ma'am. We need to confirm the identity before we write the report. If you prefer, we can ask his son, who's really next of kin."

"No, I'd better do it. I'm not sure how Frankie'd handle it. He was so full of anger when he left, but he'll still take it hard. The two of them used to be so close." Julie's voice trailed off.

After she closed the door behind the officers, Julie cuddled up next to Shadow. As the tears flowed, the dog licked the salty moisture from her cheeks. Damn the man, after all the heartache he had caused her, she had thought there were no more tears. She could hardly believe Ray was really out of her life forever. No more late night phone calls, his slurred voice pleading between his own tears. After fifteen years, their marriage was over for real.

The next morning, Saturday, Emily and Jason cried, but not as much as before, when all the arguments were going on. And not as much as when Frankie lashed out at his father as the cause of all the troubles and got a beating for his efforts. Now thirteen, Emily realized how difficult the situation had been. Even Jason at ten refused to talk about Ray when he left.

Julie had tried but hadn't kept house to the same meticulous standards established by Ray's first wife. Nor did she defer meekly to all his decisions, which he had accepted early in their marriage. When Frankie reached the rebellious teens, Ray took up drinking instead of dealing with it. During one of their arguments, he ended up shouting at Julie for taking Frankie's side. Ray said, "If his mother were alive, things would be different."

What Julie heard was "things would be better." But she was who she was and couldn't become something she wasn't. She tried favorite recipes her predecessor had cooked, but her attempts never measured up to memories of the original. Three young faces watched their father grumble about too much salt or overcooked meat. Many times Frankie took the younger two upstairs when Julie broke down into tears and Ray silently shoveled in his food.

And then Ray slapped her. He had stopped off at a bar after work, as he did more and more frequently without calling. The children had already eaten and were upstairs doing homework. Ray complained about the dried up pork chops and soggy potatoes. Julie dared to respond, "They were fine an hour ago." That was the first blow. The back of his left hand slammed across her cheek. The force and unexpectedness of the blow nearly knocked her over. The edge of the diamond on his wedding ring drew blood. Shocked, both of them froze.

"Jewel, I'm sorry." Ray's speech was suddenly serious.

Julie didn't answer. Turning, she pushed past Frankie, who was standing in the kitchen doorway. She ran upstairs and locked herself in the bathroom, choking back sobs. She rubbed cold water over her cheek, trying to erase the results of the blow. How could she face Emily and Jason? What would she tell them? More importantly, what would she do about Ray?

Raised voices of Ray and his son came through the floor. Poor Frankie, he idolized his father, despite his defiance. Then she heard footsteps on the stairs, heading first to Emily's room and then Jason's. She heard Frankie's voice but couldn't distinguish the words. How long could she hide in the bathroom?

Finally, Emily's voice called through the door. "Mom? Are you okay?"

"Fine, honey. I'll be out soon. Finish your homework."

"Unlock the door, Mom. Please."

When Julie opened the door, her daughter flew into her arms and burst into tears.

"Ssh," Julie whispered as she stroked brown hair so like Ray's. "It's okay."

"It's not okay," said Emily, rubbing her eyes. "Frankie says Dad hit you and now he's gone out. And Frankie says he's moving out 'cause he's the cause of it all."

Julie closed her eyes and took a deep breath. How was she going to fix this broken family? It seemed beyond her power, but she had to try.

Unfortunately, Julie had no control over Ray's drinking. He could go for weeks without stopping off with the guys. Then something would set him off, and he'd drink steadily for days.

Frankie moved out when he turned eighteen, and Julie finally tired of the uncertainty. Would Ray be sober or not? And if not, when would he hit her again?

They had tried a trial separation. Sometimes he turned up sober to visit Emily and Jason, often taking them to a ballgame or movie. More often he came later, after bolstering himself with liquid courage, whining and then yelling for Julie to give him another chance. Julie decided to file for a divorce the night Ray lifted his hand in anger, although he stopped himself before landing a blow. He agreed not to contest it but continued his pleading.

So now Ray was gone for good. There would be no more demands, no more pleading.

Perhaps she and Emily and Jason could try to live normal lives. Perhaps she should try contacting Frankie. How could she do it?

The police saved her the trouble and gave her his phone number. She wanted to call him but put it off. What could she say?

Frankie made the first overture. Two days later, the doorbell rang while the kids were walking Shadow. Opening the door, Julie faced a haggard-looking Frankie and a young blonde woman who looked no older than fifteen-year-old Emily.

Frankie spoke first. "I hope you don't mind us coming by without calling first, but I...."

His voice failed him.

Julie opened the door. "Did the police tell you?"

"Yeah, they tracked me down. Said you did the identification. Thanks, I don't know if I could have done it."

Unsure of his reaction, she held back the hug she wanted to give. She remembered the withdrawn six-year-old facing his father's new wife. "Please, come in."

Seated on the sofa, the two young people held hands. Frankie again took the initiative.

"Julie, this is Anne, my wife. Anne, this is..."

"I know, this is Jewel," said a musical voice. "I can't tell you how much I've longed to meet you."

"My fault," admitted Frankie. "I didn't want to get in the middle again. I hoped maybe you and Dad could work it out if I wasn't here."

Julie smiled. "Don't you realize yet that it wasn't your fault? Nor was it Emily, nor Jason. No, I'm afraid your father and I just grew apart, and he couldn't accept that we were such different people than we had been as newlyweds. And he couldn't fight demon alcohol."

The back door slammed and voices called out, "Who's here?"

"Come see," called Julie.

Emily and Jason entered, followed by Shadow. The big black dog lumbered into the room and over to Frankie, his tail wagging.

"Hi, fella, so you remember me."

The dog leaned closer to the hand scratching behind his ears. Habit prevailed, and he tried to climb on the sofa. Frankie and Anne squeezed close together, enabling the dog to enjoy his usual spot but with his head in Frankie's lap.

An awkward silence was broken by several voices all trying to speak at once.

Julie said, "Congratulations on your...."

Frankie said, "I'm sorry we didn't invite...."

Emily said, "We missed you...."

Jason just sat on the floor next to the sofa, smiling.

After general laughter, Julie asked, "Have you thought about a funeral?"

Frankie shook his head. "I don't know what to do."

"Merryman's is good. I thought a simple service at the funeral home, since there's no other family and he didn't have many friends."

The unspoken thought came to Julie that the only ones were his drinking buddies.

Frankie said, "And he'll be buried next to my mother, of course. He bought a double plot after she died."

Julie nodded. She had no objection. The one who did surprised her.

"No!" shouted Jason. "He was my dad, too. What about me and Emily? He was our dad, too."

Frankie looked surprised. "Now, Tiger,...."

"Don't you 'tiger' me! You lost your right to call me that when you moved out. First you left, then Dad, and now he's gone for good. He'll never take me fishing again." Jason burst into tears and ran from the room.

Frankie got up to follow, but Julie shook her head. "Let him cry. He needs to come to terms with Ray's death."

Emily spoke up. "But he did have a point. If you take him, we'll have nothing left of Dad. He was good to us, you know that."

"I know," Frankie admitted. "I wish I had another idea, but Dad always planned to lie in that plot next to my mother. Since the divorce," he looked at Julie with sadness rather than anger in his eyes, "your mom has no more claim on him. Don't you see that?"

"But I have a claim, and so does Jason." Emily crossed her arms and glared at her stepbrother.

Frankie's wife spoke up. "I have an idea. Frankie, did your father have anything against cremation?"

Frankie stared at her. "We never talked about it. No, I guess not. Why?"

"Suppose he were cremated. Then you could bury half of his remains next to your mother," she clasped his hand tightly, "and the other half could be put into one of those urns for Emily and Jason to have. They could keep it on a shelf or sprinkle it somewhere."

Emily's frown dissipated, turning into a smile. Frankie nodded and patted Anne's hand.

Julie said, "Frankie, you chose a very wise woman for your wife. I hope you listen to her often."

"I do. I learned more from you than you'd expect."

Emily giggled. "Now Daddy can be in two places at the same time. I think he'd like that, don't you?"

K. E. Swope

Funeral Junkie

Standing in the doorway, Charlie scanned the line of mourners in the receiving line. Good, no one he knew.

His eyes passed to his real focus, the woman standing at the end. Her brunette hair was conservatively styled in waves just below her ear lobes, possibly her natural color. Her tasteful black dress covered a body that was acceptable—not too thin and not too fat. From where Charlie stood, he guessed she wasn't too tall, either. So far, so good. Ever hopeful, he had been disappointed before, but this time he could be lucky. It was time for him to make his move.

Before heading into the viewing room, Charlie stopped in front of a convenient mirror to make certain he was looking his best. He had retained a thick head of hair into his forties, with a hint of distinguished gray at the temples. Charlie straightened the maroon handkerchief in his jacket pocket, carefully chosen to match his tie. He was ready to meet his audience.

Passing the coffin was routine. Charlie paused, turned toward it, and dipped his head respectfully for a few seconds. Just long enough to indicate he was an acquaintance only, not a close friend. The line moved slowly ahead of him, but he was in no hurry. He spent the time noting that only three other people besides the widow stood in the receiving line. From the obituary, Charlie knew the young woman would be the only daughter, the young man her husband, and the gray-haired man next to the widow could be either of the deceased man's brothers. No other survivors had been mentioned, but that didn't mean the man's wife didn't have siblings. *I've got to remember this dead man has a name, Jack Dalton, if I'm going to make this work.*

At last the line moved, and Charlie was standing in front of the young man.

"So sorry for your loss," Charlie mumbled.

The young man nodded, his eyes glazed over. Charlie could tell that he was here only for the sake of formality.

Charlie took more time with the daughter.

"I'm sorry about your father," he said, squeezing softly the hand she offered. "Jack was so proud of you."

She smiled but looked confused. "Thank you. Do I know you?"

Charlie shook his head. "I'm Charlie Watson, a business associate of your father. I didn't know him well, though, because he usually consulted one of our other advisors. The few times I met with him, our small talk revolved around your accomplishments."

"Thank you for coming," she said, already turning to the person behind him.

The gray-haired man who was next in line studied Charlie's face as he firmly grasped the visitor's hand. "I don't believe we've met."

"I met your brother when he consulted our firm about funding for a project."

"And which project was that?"

Charlie's stomach trembled. *Uh oh, this brother was part of the dead man's business. I'll have to be careful.* Charlie put on his most disarming smile and shrugged. "I'm sorry, I don't really like to discuss business at a time like this. Are you Sam?"

The man relaxed his grip. "No, I'm Ted, Jack's business partner as well as his baby brother. But you're right. This isn't the time or place to talk business. Here, let me at least give you my card."

He pulled an embossed piece of cardboard from an inside pocket of his jacket. At Charlie's raised eyebrows, his face reddened. He made as if to put the card back but then placed it in Charlie's hand instead.

"I'm just trying to salvage my father's dream," Ted replied

He turned to the widow, who had just released the hand of the woman she'd been talking with at great length. He said, "This is a business associate of Jack's. Oh, I didn't catch your name."

Charlie grasped the woman's gloved hand in both of his and looked directly into a pair of clear though watery gray eyes. If the woman had used makeup, it was tastefully and lightly done, because no black mascara tracks blazed trails through heavily powdered cheeks. He preferred the natural look in women, and his future wife couldn't be a painted doll.

"I'm Charlie Watson, Mrs. Dalton. I'm so sorry for your loss. Jack was a good person, from what I knew of him."

"Thank you for coming, Mr. Watson," she replied. Her voice was in a medium range, neither harshly shrill nor rasping. If there was one thing Charlie couldn't stand, it was a whiny woman's voice that grated on his spine like fingernails scraping across a chalkboard. He could spend time with this woman without being irritated.

The woman continued. "Did you know Jack well?"

Charlie shook his head. "No, I only dealt with him a few times. Usually someone else took care of his inquiries."

"Then it's especially kind of you to pay your respects to someone you hardly knew."

Oops, I'm starting to lose this one. She's almost too perfect—height, weight, looks, eyes—too many good things going on, so I can't blow it. An idea came to him from his internet research.

Charlie tried to look sheepish. "Well, my college major was art history, like your daughter's choice. I told Jack I hoped he didn't feel disappointed in her because she decided to go in a different direction than his business."

"I'm not sure your words helped."

Charlie shrugged. "I had to try. I never got my father to accept my own rebellion against family tradition. I ended up in business after his death, so he never knew."

"I'm sorry."

"Shouldn't I be saying that to you?"

The man behind Charlie cleared his throat loudly. Charlie nodded to the widow and walked away. Mission accomplished, first contact, so he didn't bother talking with anyone else.

While driving home, he reviewed the evening. On the whole, this relationship had strong potential. There had been so few lately. One woman had clearly dyed her hair a flaming red, a deceptive move Charlie hated. Another one sobbed uncontrollably into a sodden handkerchief, sounding like a horse with bronchitis, so he knew he wouldn't try to follow up on that one. He didn't bother with women who were too fat, too skinny, too tall; those who didn't seem to care about their appearance and those who cared too much. His search was very selective, looking for the perfect woman to become his wife.

As he neared fifty, Charlie was beginning to think something was missing from his life—companionship. It had become much clearer when he was laid off. Suddenly all his hard work, time and energy, that he had spent to become successful seemed wasted. He was accustomed to a certain lifestyle and had no desire to change now. For the short term he was in good shape, but without a decent job, the future was uncertain.

For six months he searched for work, part of the terms of receiving unemployment benefits. His skills and abilities seemed too specialized to find an easy fit. When his undergraduate degree in his first love, art history, had proved to be unmarketable, he did what so many other young men in his generation did—he got an MBA. With his knack for analysis, he climbed a narrow ladder as a financial adviser for people interested in art as investments. With the booming economy, he soared like a hot air balloon without any ballast. Eventually he reached his goal: he was in line to become the youngest vice president in the history of the investment fund where he worked.

Then the economy tanked. People retrenched with their investments, having much less if any disposable income to throw at Charlie. The general manager, in order to save the company from oblivion, "right-sized" by letting go their upper level analysts.

Charlie was more fortunate than his peers. He had no debt or family to provide for. By himself, he felt he could weather the recession sweeping the country. On his way to the top, he had bought a house and paid off the mortgage quickly. The Jaguar and the neoimpressionist art he owned were not shared with a bank. Charlie didn't want to start selling off the treasures he had collected so painstakingly. Thus he had decided to find a wife, one with some money of her own so they could live comfortably together,

A Fleeting Glimpse

Charlie wanted to follow up on this latest possibility for wife material as soon as possible. He checked the obituary for the location of Jack Dalton's funeral service, the church where he planned to accidentally see the widow again. On Sunday he went to Mass for the first time in years; his mother had dragged him there every week until he rebelled. He arrived early enough to find a choice seat near the back, off to one side so he could observe without being too obvious. Just as the priest began to chant the first part of the liturgy, Mrs. Dalton came in alone. Grace, her name is Grace, thought Charlie. She walked forward to take an empty seat near the front. The women on either side of her took turns leaning over and whispering to her. The priest spared a glance their way before continuing with the Alleluia.

After the service, Charlie stayed in his seat while the rest of the parishioners left the church. As he expected, no one bothered to talk with him. On the other hand, Grace was caught up in first one small group of women and then another. As the last group passed his pew, Charlie heard a woman say, "I don't suppose you'll come to the women's prayer meeting."

Charlie's intended lifted her chin and grimaced at her accuser. "Isn't church where I should be when I'm troubled?"

Aha, another clue. Charlie must have made a sound or moved, because just then Grace looked right at him. A slight smile passed her lips as the other women walked away. She came over to Charlie.

"Mr. Watson, isn't it?" she said, stretching out her gloved hand.

"I'm surprised you remember me," he replied, giving her hand a gentle squeeze before releasing it.

Her smile remained, forcing a dimple on one cheek to break out. "Oh, I remember you. In fact, Ted and I had a brief conversation about you just last night."

Uh, oh, the nosy brother. This could be trouble. "My ears didn't ring, so I guess it wasn't too bad."

The dimple got deeper. "Oh, it was bad enough. Ted checked up on you."

Charlie felt himself shrinking inside. He hoped all his years as a financial adviser allowed him to keep a noncommittal look on his face. All he could venture to say was, "Oh?"

Her voice turned serious. "Jack never consulted you for any financial advice. Did you even know my husband at all?"

Charlie decided it was time to cut his losses and move on. And this prospect had seemed so promising just a short while earlier. "Actually, I didn't. I'm sorry, because he was probably a good man." He turned to leave.

"Oh, yes, the world thought he was a very good man." The acid in her voice made Charlie turn back to face her. "Don't get me wrong, he never abused me. He was just so wrapped up in that damned business of his that I didn't exist for him these past ten years except for my money."

Charlie didn't know what to say. His face must have betrayed him.

"Don't look so shocked," she said. "Haven't you ever heard a woman swear before?"

"Not in church."

Grace actually let out a laugh. Luckily the church had emptied by this time. "There isn't any money, you know, so you've wasted your time. His business is struggling, and Ted's working hard to salvage the company their father started fifty years ago."

Charlie felt a sinking sensation deep inside. All his groundwork on this woman had been for nothing, and she had seemed such a promising prospect.

Grace continued. "He plowed every penny we had into the business. Told me that the short-term stinginess at home was worth it so we could retire in style. And look what it got him—an early retirement."

Charlie knew he should walk away and try his luck elsewhere. He couldn't quite do that yet. He said, "If you thought I was a fortune hunter, why did you stop to talk to me now?"

"Because I caught a glimpse of someone inside you other than a fortune hunter. Or were all your words lies?"

Charlie shook his head. "I only lied about meeting your husband."

Grace nodded. "I thought so."

"Look, I may be looking for a likely candidate for a relationship, but I'm not a complete cad. You seem like a nice person, and I didn't mean any harm. I hope you find peace in your future life."

He turned to walk away but almost immediately he felt a hand on his shoulder.

Grace said, "Perhaps we could discuss that future over lunch?"

Redemption

From her car in the visitor parking lot, Martha Flynn stared at the gate in the chain link fence, willing it to open. The blustery afternoon was typical of southern New England in March, with the sun struggling to fight its way past the scurrying clouds. From time to time, a raindrop, fat with the promise of spring, plopped onto the windshield. Martha seemed to remember that it had also been cloudy on the day of the accident, almost exactly five years earlier.

Just then the metal gate gave out a groan and began moving. When it had opened all the way, a solitary figure walked out, shoulders hunched and feet shuffling. Martha could tell it was her daughter by the matching denim jacket and skirt, one of her favorite outfits. Except for the clothing, the figure didn't look familiar, with the pale face and hair standing up in random spikes. Martha reminded herself to wait before asking too many questions.

Heedless of the chill air outside, Martha rolled down her window and waved.

"Hurry up, Amanda. Time to get you home."

Her daughter didn't look up, just kept shuffling forward, head down against the wind. Martha felt tears fill her eyes and quickly wiped them away. She had vowed not to cry, for this was a happy day, a homecoming.

Amanda's pace never wavered and her head didn't lift. One foot followed the other, over and over, stopping before she reached the passenger door. She made no move to open it, as if she had forgotten how to perform such a simple task. Martha reached over and opened the door from the inside. Then she started the car and turned up the heater.

"You must be chilled to the bone, dear."

Amanda got in the car and slammed the door, not saying a word.

Martha reminded herself to tread lightly. She had vowed to keep the conversation light. There would be time later to inquire about the hair. The important thing was to put the pieces of their family back together.

"Seat belt, please," urged Martha. "Remember the Flynn motto: the car won't move till the seat belt clicks."

The next moment she wished she could take back her words, anything that referred to cars or driving. Her husband often gave her grief about opening her mouth before activating her brain. When she heard the passenger seat belt click, she put the car in gear and headed for the highway.

"Just wait till you see your room. Dad painted it your favorite lilac color, and your gran made a cross-stitch throw pillow that says….Oops, I almost let the secret out. She wants it to be a surprise."

No response.

"You'll really like the new house. Of course, it's smaller than the other one. I haven't met too many of the neighbors yet, but I haven't had time."

Still no response.

Martha regretted her words almost as soon as they left her mouth. Her therapist had told her to refrain from references to the past as much as possible at first. It was just too hard to remember all the admonitions. She tried again to find a safe topic.

"Dad's in Boston on business, but he'll be back Friday night. He said to tell you he's sorry he couldn't be here to drive you home."

This brought out what sounded suspiciously like a laugh. Glancing over, Martha saw her daughter was still staring straight ahead.

"Got your hair cut? It looks, well, different."

"Yeah, awful."

At last, a response. The therapist had told her it would take time for Amanda to open up and feel comfortable after being inside prison walls. Martha was trying to ease the tension she felt in the only way she knew how, with chatter.

"I thought hair stylists have to be trained to get a license."

This statement was greeted with wild laughter.

"Mom, the so-called hair stylist was my cell mate. She had her bitches hold me down in the shower so she could hack at my hair with a razor. She said it was my getting-out gift."

Martha winced at the words. "That's terrible! Didn't any guards know?"

"Probably their entertainment for the day."

"That's just not right. Couldn't you complain to someone?"

Amanda let out a derisive snort of laughter. "Yeah, I guess I could have. Of course, there would have been an inquiry, and then where do you suppose I'd be? Certainly not here with you."

Martha was silent for a moment. Then she said cheerfully, "Well, I'll call Greta and see if she can fit you in sometime soon. She can work magic with her scissors."

"Whatever."

Silence descended on the car.

"Did I tell you Kenny got a summer job at the Clam Shack? On his days off, he plans to be a lifeguard at the yacht club. He says he needs to save up because college textbooks are terribly expensive."

"How nice for him," said Amanda, her voice cracking.

Martha winced. Another sharp reminder of what her daughter had missed—no high school graduation, just a GED and a few college courses brought to the inmates by the local community college. No matter how hard she tried, she couldn't seem to find a safe topic. She really wanted to connect with her daughter again. Visits had been too short for a real conversation, and the glass partition prevented any comforting hugs. The only time she remembered Amanda saying much was about the horse-rescue project at the prison. Maybe that would help to get a conversation going.

"I was thinking about that horse. What was its name? I forgot."

"What?"

"You know, that horse you told me you worked with, the one that had been nearly dead from starvation and neglect."

Still nothing. When Martha glanced over, though, her daughter was still staring straight ahead, her jaw clenched.

Hoping for more of a response, she tried again. "It was Molly, wasn't it?"

"Uh-huh." That sounded reluctant.

At their visits, Amanda had seemed alive only when she mentioned that horse. Perhaps it reminded her of the riding lessons she had once enjoyed. A lifetime ago.

After several moments of silence, Amanda spoke without being prompted. "It's okay, Mom. You don't have to make conversation."

When Martha glanced over, she saw sadness on her passenger's face.

Amanda's voice was almost a whisper. "It's never completely silent in there. Even at night, there were snores and footsteps of guards, even yelling. Really, it's okay not to talk."

Relieved, Martha concentrated on her driving. It would be easier once they got home, surrounded by familiar things, even though the house itself was different.

When Martha noticed something she wanted to point out to her daughter, she quickly stifled the impulse and kept quiet, saving the thought for a time Amanda was ready to talk. It certainly wouldn't do for her to have an accident because of inattention, today of all days.

The thirteen miles passed quietly and all too slowly for Martha's comfort level. She hoped that once they reached the house that Amanda would be more comfortable. Finally, they reached the new neighborhood, toward their much smaller house.

"I hope you're not too disappointed, dear," said Martha, as she turned in their new street.

Amanda sighed. "Mom, really, stop trying so hard."

As she unlocked the front door, Martha gestured for her daughter to enter first. "Well, here we are."

Amanda walked in and glanced around at the small living room to the left, just inside the door. Martha closed her eyes briefly, remembering the other home with its large open foyer, shiny hardwood floors, and chandelier gleaming its welcome. This is here, this is now, she mumbled softly to herself as the therapist had suggested.

Amanda hadn't seemed to notice. She just stood there, with a blank look. She finally looked up the open stairway.

"Your room is on the right, Kenny's across from you, and Dad and I are in the back. I put towels on your bed. Would you like something to eat?"

Amanda shook her head and started for the stairs. "I'd just like to lie down for a while."

"I'll call you when supper's ready. It's just you and me, since Dad's away and Kenny has a late practice."

"Don't bother. I'm more tired than hungry. Maybe I'll just get something later."

Martha reached out as if to hug her daughter, but pulled back from this stranger.

Amanda looked up, and smiled, just a shadow of her former wide-open grin. "Mom, you don't have to wait on me. Let me get used to the change. I'll help myself. Okay?"

"Okay."

Martha watched her eldest child climb the stairs, wondering how they could meld their family back together. She decided to keep her hands busy, hoping to keep her thoughts on the lasagna she had made as a welcome meal. At least it would be good reheated, too.

She had just taken the pan out of the oven when the back door opened. She heard a thud in the back entry. Evidently Kenny was home.

He came in, sniffing deeply.

"Wow, lasagna. You haven't made that in a long time. What's the occasion?"

Martha slapped him playfully on his upper arm.

"You know well enough that your sister came home today."

"Yeah? Where is she?"

"Upstairs, having a good sleep, I hope."

"How'd it go?"

Martha shrugged. "Not too badly, I suspect. What am I saying? I don't have any idea how to reconnect with her. We used to be so close."

"Mom, how can things ever be the same? We've all changed."

"But not for the better. We moved to a smaller house, your father travels too much for the extra money, and I have to stand over a hot grill at Casertano's. And you're headed for State U. instead of Duke, the way you'd planned."

Kenny shrugged, an unconscious copy of his father. "It's probably better this way. I'll get more playing time, probably be one of the starting five on the court as a freshman. At Duke, I'd be just another good but not great basketball player on the bench most of the time. Besides, State has the courses I need and were willing to fork over some financial help."

Martha turned to brush away a tear. Her son seemed to accept their lack of extra money after paying all those fees to the defense lawyers. She had accepted that she had to work; her husband had accepted the extra effort at his job. Now Amanda needed to find some acceptance.

"Go put your practice clothes in the washer while I set the table and make a salad."

Soon she had tossed some greens with tomatoes, green peppers, and radishes, adding a hint of oil. By the time the salad was ready, she heard the washer start up.

It was a quiet meal, like so many others since Amanda had been gone. Kenny had his nose in his social science book, while he forked big bites of food into his mouth. Just another normal evening loomed ahead with one subtle difference—Martha's thoughts kept turning to her daughter, asleep upstairs.

After the dishes were done, she called Greta to ask if she had any openings the next day. At first Greta said she was full, but when Martha explained the situation, she sighed.

"Just bring her by about 5:30. That's when my last customer is done."

"Thanks, you're a real gem. I owe you."

"Well, you deserve some positive stuff in your life after what your family's been through."

Martha felt tears sting her eyes as she hung up. Yes, her family could certainly use some good days. Then she had an inspiration and made one more phone call.

After watching the news, Martha headed up the stairs to bed. At her daughter's closed door, she hesitated, tempted to knock. Then she decided to let the poor girl alone. Sleep was supposed to be the great healer, along with time. She hoped her family could reap the benefits from both.

During the night, Martha got up to go to the bathroom. When she went out into the hall, she saw by the bathroom's nightlight, that her daughter's door was open. From the top of the stairs, she saw a light downstairs. She hesitated, not wanting to intrude, but her mothering instincts kicked in and she walked slowly down the stairs.

Amanda stood at the refrigerator door, looking inside.

"Are you hungry?" asked Martha quietly.

Her daughter jumped. "Geez, Mom, you startled me. Yeah, my stomach woke me up with its rumblings. What's to eat?"

"I made lasagna, and it won't take long to reheat. I think Kenny left some salad, too."

Martha moved toward the refrigerator, but her daughter didn't move away from where she blocked the opening.

"Mom, I'd really rather help myself, okay? Why don't you go back to bed. I promise I won't make a mess."

"Actually, I think I'll have some milk since I'm up."

Martha poured herself a glass of milk and sat down at the table.

Amanda pulled out the lasagna and the salad, but then stood there with her hands full. "Uh, Mom, where are the microwave dishes?"

Martha jumped up to get them, but her daughter frowned. So Martha instead told her where to find the things she needed. It was so hard just to sit there, but she forced herself to watch as her daughter helped herself. She remembered Amanda as a two-year-old insisting that she could feed herself. Those were the innocent days, long gone.

As she ate slowly, Amanda seemed to be chewing each bite at least twenty times.

"Is the food okay?" Martha finally asked. "You're eating so slowly."

"It's just as delicious as I remembered. Plus, it's great to eat without worrying that the bell will ring before I'm done eating."

"Oh," said Martha, not knowing what to say. A novelty for her.

"It's just that everything was so regulated in there," said Amanda, waving her fork around in the air. "I want to move at my own speed instead of lock step according to someone else's schedule."

She looked at her mother firmly. "Please tell me you don't have every minute planned for me."

Martha let out a chuckle. "No, I haven't done that. The only thing I have scheduled is a haircut appointment for you tomorrow at 5:30 with Greta."

She saw Amanda wince.

Her daughter said, "I don't know if I'm ready to meet other people."

"You'll be after her last customer."

Amanda let out a relieved sigh. "Okay, then. I have to admit it will be nice to have a good haircut, although I don't know if there's enough to do anything with."

"Oh, Greta's amazing. She'll have you looking neat and trim. You'll see."

They sat in silence for another ten minutes. Then a clattering on the stairs announced the arrival of another person. Kenny came into the kitchen like a whirlwind.

"I thought I smelled food," he said sniffing appreciatively. "Did you leave any?"

Amanda looked up at him. "My god, you're a giant! You didn't look so big when you visited and were sitting down."

Instead of answering, her brother grabbed her from behind and lifted her off the chair.

"Stronger, too. Coach has us lifting weights to improve our upper body strength."

"Put me down, you oaf!"

Kenny dropped her. "Your wish is my command. As long as there's more lasagna."

Martha jumped up to warm up a big piece for her son.

Amanda looked at her strangely. Then she said, "Mom, why don't you let him do it himself."

Kenny laughed. "Because she's afraid I'll eat all of what's left, that's why."

All three shared a laugh. Martha felt good inside.

A minute later, the good feeling disappeared.

"Hey, sis, are you coming to the game tonight? We're playing Mansfield for the last regular season game before the playoffs."

There was dead silence in the room. Amanda looked down at her plate, Martha's stomach clenched, but Kenny took another big bite. Then he looked up, as if realizing his goof.

"Oops," he said, but didn't sound apologetic. "I'm sorry if I brought up a sore subject, but basketball is important to me and I can't pretend otherwise."

Martha's mind went back to five years ago. Strange, most of the details of that day were gone from her memory. It had seemed so ordinary, just another day in the life of her active family. That evening, she and Jim took then twelve-year-old son Kenny to the high school basketball tournament. For the first time ever, their team seemed to be headed for the state championship. Amanda, a high-school senior, drove to pick up her best friend Cindy so they could go to the game together.

After the game she dropped off Cindy. Amanda said she stopped at the end of the street and looked both ways before making the left hand turn for home. She looked left and then right, before pulling out. She agreed she should have looked left one more time, because that quickly a car traveling at what police later said was over eighty miles an hour came around the bend. It hit Amanda's car on the front left bumper and spun it around. The impact sent the other car out of control, sending it careening into a tree. The driver died. Amanda's seat belt saved her from serious injury.

Kenny's words brought back those dark days—Amanda's arrest, the charges of pulling out into traffic, and the subsequent trial. Without any witnesses, the prosecutor set up a relatively new teenaged driver as unsafe because the other car had the right of way. Because the investigating officer never gave her a breathalyzer test, the prosecutor hinted that Amanda had been under the influence. Lawyers dithered and talked, but in the end the jury found Amanda at fault—involuntary manslaughter. Initially she was supposed to serve ten years, but with good behavior only five years were carved out of their family's life. Five years lost.

Now, Martha had no words now to smooth over any hard feelings. She was so tired of feeling sad, of feeling life was unfair. She took the coward's way out and went to bed, hoping to sleep. As she climbed the stairs, she heard low voices from the kitchen. She smiled to herself. Maybe the two siblings could break the ice.

In the morning, Martha found the dishes from the midnight meal all neatly washed and stacked by the sink. She saw Kenny off to school and got ready for her daytime shift at the restaurant. Before she left, she wrote a quick note to tell Amanda where she could find fixings for lunch.

Luckily the restaurant was busy, not just for breakfast, brunch and lunch, but well into the afternoon. Even if she'd wanted to call Amanda to check on her, which she knew she shouldn't do, she was too busy in the kitchen to take the time.

By the time Martha got home, she barely had time for a shower before it was time to leave for Greta's salon. She waved at Amanda, who was lounging in front of an old movie on TV, and told her she'd be ready soon.

As promised, the parking lot was empty when they got there, with one car leaving. Greta frowned at the ruin of Amanda's hair.

"At least you've got some hair left," she said. "I was afraid you'd been shaved and I'd have nothing at all to work with. Just sit down and leave it to the expert."

Amanda said nothing but did manage a smile. Martha hoped she would soon be able to interact with others.

Just then the bell at the door jingled. In dashed a tall woman with graying hair dangling down her back in a loose braid.

"Greta, darling, I'm desperate. Jim wants to go to a gala tonight and I can't do a thing with my hair."

Martha watched as Amanda seemed to shrink into herself.

"Head up," demanded Greta of Amanda, lifting her chin with one hand. "Sure, Yvonne, I'll do a French knot for you as soon as I'm done here."

"You're a life saver!" Yvonne turned to sit down, then turned back. "Say, aren't you Amanda Flynn? It's great to see you're back."

Amanda said nothing, didn't even look up at the woman.

"You remember me, don't you? You used to take riding lessons when you were little. You always sat a horse with such natural grace."

At that, Amanda glanced up with a brief smile. Then Martha saw her shut herself down again.

The tall woman sat down. The shop was silent for several moments, except for the snipping of Greta's scissors.

Yvonne suddenly looked up. "Say, Amanda, if you'd like to come by the stables, I have some new stock that I'm trying to get used to people before I use them for children's lessons."

Amanda shrugged.

"Hold still," commanded Greta, "or this will turn out worse than it was before."

Martha was tempted to jump into the conversation, but she saw Yvonne shake her head.

The tall woman continued, "A friend of mine at the prison told me about the horse rescue efforts there."

At those words, Amanda's head came up. Only to be pushed down again by Greta.

Yvonne pretended she hadn't seen the sudden interest. "She said that there's been such a great demand that they can't accept all the neglected horses being offered. She asked me if I could take four of the horses that they'd already been working with. She seemed to think one of them, a mare, had real potential as a show horse, if someone worked with her. What was that horse's name? Monkey? Mokie?"

"Molly?" asked Amanda quietly.

"That's it! Molly. I haven't had a horse with good show potential in my stable for a long time. I'd love to do something with her, but I just don't know how I could find time to spend the amount of time a new horse needs. It would be great to introduce her to the summer fair tour. I really need someone who has time to devote exclusively to her."

"I have the time," said Amanda quietly.

Martha felt herself smiling broadly. She saw a matching smile on her daughter's face. That second phone call last evening had been worth it.

K. E. Swope

A Fleeting Glimpse

Good Day, Bad Day

Sammy opened his right eye. The first rays of morning light brightened the single window in his room. A good sign, no rain. Contented, he closed his eye.

Then he opened his left eye. This time he saw gray. Oh, no, clouds, maybe rain. Maybe it won't be a good day after all.

Sighing, he opened both eyes at once and worked to focus them together on a single point, the window. The left one kept wandering away, downward along the dull gray wall of his room. Sometimes, especially first thing in the morning, his eyes didn't remember they were supposed to work together. Patiently he worked through his assigned eye exercises.

Finally his two eyes together saw only one window, full of bright sun. It promised to be a good day, after all.

He rubbed his chin to make sure his whiskers hadn't grown too much overnight. Since they started showing up more gray than brown, he had been trying to appear clean-shaven. He didn't want to look like an old man, since he had just turned forty. With his wandering morning eyes, he had started shaving at night to avoid nicking himself. Yeah, they didn't grow overnight.

Suddenly Sammy was a blur of motion. He couldn't be late for breakfast—cook had promised to make Mickey Mouse pancakes for him this morning. Somehow pancakes always tasted better that way.

None of the other residents in the dining room at Sierra Home acknowledged Sammy's entrance, too busy nibbling at their food. Sammy didn't care; he knew they weren't being unfriendly, just in their usual fog after nurse passed out morning meds. Being late meant he could taste his food this morning before going in to see nurse for his own pills.

Cook set a plate in front of Sammy.

He asked, "Do you feel like catching a mouse, Master Puss in Boots?"

Sammy just nodded, staring at his breakfast. As promised, there were two smaller circles strategically placed above one large one, which had two raisins for eyes and a strand of bacon for a mouth.

"Thanks," he said, his mouth already full of his first bite.

After seeing nurse and signing out, Sammy put on a jacket before leaving, free for the day. Sometimes he returned for lunch, but it was usually a no-taste meal, so he skipped it. He was perfectly capable of feeding himself, just not able to keep a job because he was bi-polar.

He pushed back the blue tarp. The rusted grocery cart had been discarded by the downtown grocery store because of bent wheels. Sammy didn't care if the front ones tried to go in opposite directions, like his eyes. He was strong enough to make the cart go where he wanted. The metal sides were rusted but not badly dented. He took good care of it, but he couldn't get rid of the squeak in the wheels. Every afternoon, when he returned home, he examined the hard rounded rubber for gum, nails, or other debris picked up that day. Every evening he carefully replaced the blue tarp to prevent further rusting of the metal sides. His cart was precious, something he took care to keep in working order.

Before leaving this morning, he checked to make sure he had three empty garbage bags, ready to accept his gatherings for the day. Attached to his belt so no one could steal it was his leather pouch. It held the special treasures he gathered.

His stomach comfortably full, Sammy pushed the cart out the driveway and turned right. Because it was Tuesday, trash pickup was scheduled for the north side, and he wanted to get to the bins before the town trucks passed. He coveted every empty soda and beer can, worth either five or ten cents at the gobbler-uppers at the grocery store.

On Pine Street, Mrs. Johnson waved at him from her front door.

"Yoohoo, Sammy," she called. "Would you pull my bins out to the curbing?"

A Fleeting Glimpse

Sammy waved back. "Sure," he said, before parking his cart on the sidewalk, away from passing traffic.

It took only a few moments to wheel Mrs. Johnson's cart to the curb for the morning pickup. The gray-haired woman held the door open slightly to pass over his tip, the usual dime.

"Thank you, young man," she said, making shooing motions with her hands. "You'd best hurry along to school so you don't get a detention."

Sammy smiled and said, "Thank you."

He had long ago explained to the old lady that he was way past the age to sit in school. She had to be at least a hundred years old, so everyone probably looked young to her.

One quick glance through her trash bin told him the paper bag on top was full of empty beer cans. He checked—sure enough, they were all well rinsed, almost clean enough to refill. Sammy placed the cans in his trash bag designated for "cans, metal." The gobbler-upper next to the grocery store wouldn't tolerate mixing up bottles and cans. He had quickly learned, too, that clear plastic and green plastic had to go in different machines, as did glass bottles. No wonder people don't want to do it themselves; it takes a lot of work to remember how to recycle properly.

For two more hours Sammy criss-crossed the north side of town, where many wheeled bins sat next to paper bags full of bottles and cans for him. By the time he turned toward the grocery store, his three trash bags were overflowing. He had extras in paper bags that he had carefully folded up after sorting the bottles and cans.

It was early enough in the day that the room where the gobbler-uppers accepted donations was nearly empty. One old man stood in front of the glass bottle machine, so Sammy started with the metal cans. He placed the offerings, one by one, in the mouth of the recycler god. One time he had carelessly tossed in a can, only to watch it spin aimlessly around in the long tunnel. A woman at the next machine had told him to take it out and try again, more carefully. Sammy was afraid to put his hand in that long throat—what if the machine decided to chomp down on his arm? Afraid to disobey, he gingerly reached in with his left arm and grabbed for the spinning can. He almost shut his eyes, afraid to see his blood spurting all over. Then he had the can and yanked it out before the gobbler-upper decided it wanted Sammy's arm as an offering.

Instead of trying again, he tossed the offending can in the bin full of rejects and punched the button for his receipt. He never went back to that machine again and was careful to always place his offerings reverently in the mouth of the great machine.

It was turning out to be a good day. His right eye had predicted correctly. With the money from the returnables, Sammy had enough money to buy three tins of cat food and a small bag of dry nuggets. Then it was time to turn downtown.

Along the way, Sammy picked up several more cans and bottles that had been tossed from open windows of passing cars. He also found some slivers of gold-colored glass, which he added to the pouch at his waist.

His stomach growled; time for lunch.

When he reached downtown, he watched the line of people in suits waiting impatiently for one of Joe's specials. Sammy could imagine the taste of every bite being devoured. Much as he wanted to rush in, he knew he had to wait until all the business people had been served their hot dogs and kielbasa. Joe added cheese, chili, or sauerkraut, as his customers desired, but Sammy preferred just mustard. He especially liked the ones with hard blackened outsides.

Sammy watched jealously as the pile of cooked meat slowly disappeared in exchange for dollar bills. He knew Joe's system and liked when it didn't work. Over the years, Joe had figured out about how many pieces to cook ahead and keep warm at the side of his grill. That way he could serve up a fast meal for all his business customers in a hurry to get back to their desks. Because the meal crowd came in waves, Joe learned to cook the franks and spicy sausages in batches. After the first wave, he started with fresh meat. Sometimes a few stayed on the side, getting darker and darker, until they became too well-cooked to serve.

After the second wave of customers had passed, Sammy knew it was time to make his move. Pushing the cart across the street, he announced his arrival with the wheels going "squeak, squeal."

As usual, Joe ignored his presence until Sammy spoke.

"Hi, Joe."

While scraping off the grill but not looking up, Joe replied, "Hi, Sammy."

Sammy tried to focus on the grill. One eye wanted to look up at the sky when the other one looked down, so he wasn't sure if anything was left on the grill.

Sammy asked, "Good business today?"

"Yep."

Joe wasn't making it easy. He usually didn't, so Sammy tried to think of something else to say before getting to the point. After all, he had learned some manners in his forty years.

"Think it'll rain later, wind's coming from the east."

"Maybe," said Joe, still scraping away on what seemed to be a mighty clean grill.

"I heard some sirens a while back," ventured Sammy, scratching his head just under the fringe of reddish hair circling an otherwise bare scalp.

"That so?"

"Seen any action?"

"Nope."

This was getting hard. Sammy moved his weight from one foot to the other, reaching up to scratch his chin.

Joe stopped scraping and turned his head to look at Sammy, his eyes twinkling and the corners of his mouth turned up in a grin. "I did see an ambulance heading toward the hospital early this morning, though."

"Oh," said Sammy, nodding wisely. "That musta been the ones I heard. Probably another truck jack-knifed on the highway."

Joe turned back to concentrate on his grill, spreading a thin layer of oil over the solid plate. The late lunch crowd would be coming by soon, just as hungry as the early birds.

Sammy's stomach let out a rumble, not quite a growl but more than a groan.

He finally got to the point. "Any burnt ones?"

"Yep," said Joe, pulling out two thick blackened cylinders. "Your favorite, the spicy ones."

"How much?"

"Twenty cents."

Sammy opened his bags. "I got two Pepsis, a Dr. Pepper, and a Budweiser."

He handed three cans and a bottle to the vendor, who put them in a paper sack. Sometimes he was careless and forgot to take that sack with him, so Sammy always checked back before going back to Sierra Home.

Sammy placed his lunch on top of the cart and moved away. He knew to stay out of the way of Joe's important customers. He found an empty park bench in one corner of the small park overlooking the ocean inlet. While he chewed on his kielbasa, liberally slathered with mustard, Sammy watched two sailboats sliding through the water. Despite his jacket, he shivered. How can people enjoy being out there in September? He remembered going for a boat ride when he was little, how the wind seemed stronger without trees around to stop its ferocious attack. He zipped up his oversized windbreaker that barely came together over his abdomen.

All too soon his lunch was finished. He threw the two paper napkins in a nearby trash bin. From habit, he used a stick to poke around, looking for empty bottles or cans. No luck; someone else was already there. Sammy shrugged. He wasn't greedy—there were enough containers in other places.

Sammy pushed his cart down Ocean Avenue toward Fern's Treasure Shop, the wheels going "squeak, squeal" over the sidewalk. He parked it in the doorway of the empty store next door, out of the way of pedestrians. Usually no one bothered an apparently abandoned cart, but he didn't want to look for another.

Before going into Fern's store, he pulled out a handful of treasures from the leather pouch at his waist. He rolled the brightly colored glass pieces around in his beefy hands, admiring the way they sparkled in the sun. Some showed jagged edges but most were worn smooth from being rolled around in the surf. Fern would be pleased. He carefully replaced the shards in his leather pouch, picked up the bag of cat food out of the cart, and headed for Fern's store.

He was nearly knocked over by a broad-shouldered man wearing dreadlocks, who rushed past carrying a bright red tie-dyed tee-shirt. Sammy leaned into the wall so he wouldn't fall. His left eye refused to follow the right, so he shut the left eyelid to see his feet more clearly. Placing one foot carefully on the single step, Sammy opened the door and walked into a cloud of odors, the usual incense and scented candles. He breathed deeply and then sneezed once, loudly.

With his air waves cleared, he crossed to the left side of the shop where chimes hung from the ceiling. One at a time, he tapped them gently to start the chorus of praise—first the hollow wood reeds, then the thin silvery tubes, and finally the long brass cylinders. Closing his eyes and breathing deeply, Sammy imagined he was in heaven.

A voice called softly from the rear of the store. "Well, my friend, you don't look quite so yellow today."

Sammy smiled without opening his eyes. "Good. Feeling green."

As dainty footsteps approached, Sammy opened his eyes. The top of Fern's head reached barely to his chin, and her long gray hair pulled back in an intricate braid revealed one pointed ear that she said marked her to be of elven heritage. Sammy wasn't sure about that, but he believed that she could see auras, the way she claimed. When she saw yellow around him, she knew it was one of his bad days, but today he was feeling good.

"Bet the guy that just left is red, though."

Fern's hazel eyes closed briefly. "No, that one's muddy. He'll soon do something very stupid and very violent."

"You should tell someone."

"What should I say? 'That one's troubled and bound to commit an atrocious and vicious act?' The police have their eye on him for little things, but they can't arrest a sociopath before he actually hurts someone."

Sammy patted her on the shoulder. "Isn't easy, is it?"

The little woman shook her head, and then forced a smile. "Ah, but I have my friends, don't I? And the spirits comfort me."

Sammy set down the bag of cat food.

"Here's some food for Dust Bunny," he said, looking around for the kitten. "Where is she?"

Fern waved one hand in the air, the gems on her finger rings catching the flicker from a nearby candle. "Here and there."

Sammy tried not to look too disappointed. He had found the tiny creature in a garbage bin behind a Japanese restaurant. At first he didn't know what the clotted mat of black fur was until it said, "Meow." Then it opened a pair of wide greenish-yellow eyes, and Sammy was in love.

Because pets weren't allowed at Sierra House, he had asked Fern to adopt the kitten, with a promise to help buy food for it. He looked forward to visits to 'his' kitten, but often he was disappointed that Dust Bunny didn't always come out from the day's hiding place to see him.

"Try not to take it personally," said Fern. "That one is a free spirit."

Sammy sighed. Then he patted the leather pouch. "Got some more sparklies for you."

Fern clapped her hands, her eyes bright and shining like the glass shards. "I'm so pleased. I used all the ones you brought me last week. Come see what I made."

She took his pudgy hand in her tiny one and led him to the rack of jewelry hanging in the front window. Colored glass and beads formed pendants and bracelets and anklets that caught the eye of tourists walking along the sidewalk. Nearby hung three dream-catchers, looking like spider webs that trapped light and colors instead of insects in their yarn webbing. Among the strands, Fern had tied feathers and beads. One about the size of a saucer in shades of blue caught Sammy's attention. He reached out to finger the soft down of owl feathers intermingled with blue yarn and sapphire glass.

Fern nodded. "Blue appeals to you, does it?"

Sammy shrugged but he couldn't take his gaze off the ornament. Somehow both of his eyes were cooperating to focus on the interwoven strands. "I guess," was all he said.

"Your inner eye is awakening then."

Sammy turned toward his friend. His eyes began their unfocused dance, so Fern also danced around in his view, although she was standing still.

"Think so?"

"Perhaps," she replied. "Let's have some tea."

Soon the two of them sat comfortably in a pair of wicker chairs facing a table on which sat a fat candle, two mugs, and a teapot. After pouring out the tea to cool slightly, Fern began intoning the meditative chant she chose for this day, the third week of Virgo with Moon ascending. Sammy hummed along as best he could.

The bell over the shop's doorway tinkled. Fern got up to tend her customers.

"See if you can continue without me while you sip your tea," she said before gliding away.

Sammy breathed in the scent of the candle and listened to soft music playing on Fern's disc player. Hammer dulcimer, he thought, before losing himself in the melody. At one point, a small black body jumped on his lap, turned around three times, and kneaded his thigh before curling up for a sleep. One plaintive "Meow" made her demands known, so Sammy began automatically rubbing under her chin.

He jerked awake when a hand tapped him on the shoulder. Fern stood in front of him, holding out the blue dream-catcher.

"Good work, my friend," she said. "I saw traces of blue in your aura while you were relaxed. This will help you to open that third eye fully."

Sammy hung his head. "I can't pay you."

Fern opened his right hand and wrapped his stubby fingers around one edge of the dream-catcher. "You've brought me so many gifts from sea and air that I've used in my creations, so I'm sure I owe you. How about we make a bargain—take this as a gift from me and, in return, continue to bring me the treasures that you find. Deal?"

"Deal," said Sammy. "I know just where to put this—in the window of my room so I can see it before I go to sleep and first thing when I wake up."

Sammy could almost sense the good blue feeling coursing through him as he left Fern's shop. He carefully wrapped his very own dream catcher in a double layer of paper bags and stashed it under the nearly empty trash bags. Such a treasure could catch the greedy attention of passersby who would want to grab it for themselves.

It had definitely been a very good day, thought Sammy as he turned toward Sierra Home. He didn't want to be late for supper: cook was making hamburger and macaroni, one of Sammy's favorites. He could almost taste the tomato sauce as it slipped down his throat. It had been a long time since Joe's lunch, and Fern's nibblings, though healthy, didn't fill a man up the way a good solid meal of macaroni did.

Sammy checked the traffic light on the corner before stepping off the curbing. He knew the law and followed it because he didn't want to cause any trouble for anyone. Just as he pushed his cart into the pedestrian markings across Ocean Avenue, he heard a police siren and the squeal of tires. He looked up and saw a brown car coming at him like he imagined a tornado would—fast and unstoppable.

The next thing Sammy realized he was lying on his back in the street with lots of eyes staring down at him.

"He's awake," said a woman.

"Here's the ambulance," shouted a man.

Sammy tried to sit up. Hands held him down.

"Don't move," ordered a man wearing a uniform. He set down a satchel, from which he started pulling out instruments. None of them looked sharp, so Sammy relaxed.

The man started poking and prodding. When he touched Sammy's shoulder, Sammy yelled. The man put a needle in his arm, and the pain soon went away. Then two more men appeared, also in the same uniform, and together they moved him to a flat board. They loaded him into the back of an ambulance, and one of the men got inside with him.

Sammy started to feel sleepy. But he wanted one thing.

"Could you turn on the siren?" he asked before falling asleep.

The next thing Sammy knew, he was lying in a bed. It didn't feel like his own, it was stiffer. His eyes didn't want to work together, so he had to concentrate hard to see more than just white around him.

When he finally got his eyes to work together, he saw a strange woman dressed in a flowered smock leaning over his bed.

"Are you an angel?" Sammy asked.

The woman smiled. "Angels of mercy, some call us."

At Sammy's puzzled look, she continued, "I'm a nurse. You were in an accident. What do you remember?"

Sammy's eyes chose that moment to go their separate ways. He just shook his head and went back to sleep.

Someone was poking him. Sammy opened his eyes and saw a two-headed monster with a double set of eyeglasses. Each head was shiny in the overhead light.

"How are you feeling, son?" asked the monster.

Sammy squeezed his eyes shut and concentrated on his eye exercises. When he looked again, he saw a bald-headed man with only one head and one pair of glasses.

Before he replied, Sammy tried to sit up. Only then did he notice that his whole left side from the waist to his neck was encased in solid white. *I wonder if turtles feel this stiff in their shells.*

"Who? What?"

"I'm Dr. Morrissey, and I've fixed your shoulder and elbow for you."

"Why?"

"Your shoulder was dislocated, so I had to stabilize it, and your ulna was broken just below the elbow. That's why you're wrapped like a cocoon." The doctor placed a cold, round piece of metal on Sammy's chest and concentrated for a moment. "Good heart-rate. Rest is the best thing for you right now."

Sammy still felt sleepy, but he wanted to know what happened. Before the doctor could leave, Sammy reached out to grab the man's sleeve with his free hand.

"Wait. What happened?"

"You were in an accident. A speeding car ran you over while you were crossing the street. You have a dislocated shoulder and fracture of the elbow."

"I heard a siren. Was I in trouble with the police?"

"No, they were chasing a bank robber. It was the robber's car that hit you."

"Did they catch the robber?"

"I don't know."

Just as he was falling off to sleep, Sammy remembered seeing a man behind the wheel of a car heading toward his face. The man had dread locks and wore a crimson tie-dyed shirt.

"Muddy man," he mumbled as he fell asleep.

Someone was shaking him again. It was a different woman in a flowered smock. He had to think for a minute before he realized she must also be a nurse. He thought nurses wore white, but sometimes he got things confused.

"Time for your medication," she said kindly, holding out a tiny paper cup and a glass with a straw.

Sammy opened his mouth and swallowed when told. Before the nurse could leave, he asked, "What happened to my things?"

"Your clothes are in the closet, and your wallet is in the patient safe."

"No, I mean my cart?"

The nurse shook her head. "I don't know anything about a cart. Is it important?"

"It is to me."

After the nurse left, Sammy felt tears fill his eyes. He could probably find another cart, but he felt so bad that he hadn't taken care of the dream-catcher, Fern's gift to him. She'd probably never trust him again.

Just as he was wiping his eyes with the edge of the sheet, he heard a familiar voice in the hallway. It was Fern. How could he tell her he had been careless with his gift? He tried pulling the sheet over his head, to disappear, but the sheet wasn't long enough.

Fern came into his room, looking serious.

Oh, no, she's going to scold me for being careless.

Seeing he was awake, Fern studied him, a frown on her face. "You're looking mighty yellow, my friend."

Sammy swallowed and couldn't answer.

"How are you feeling?"

"Sore," said Sammy, "and sleepy."

Fern chuckled at that. "Doctors seem to think that if you sleep, the medicine will work better. They're partly right—when you sleep you give your body a chance to heal itself."

"It was the man who ran out of your shop. Where did he go?"

"The police had an easy job of it. After he hit you with his car, he lost control and hit a light pole. He was so dazed that he didn't fight when they put handcuffs on him."

"Good." Sammy yawned.

Fern grinned at him. "They're calling you a hero."

"Me? Why?"

"Because you stopped him."

Sammy tried to laugh but it hurt his insides. "I didn't stop him. He hit me."

"Well, you can press charges, if you want. Assault added to bank robbery will put him away for a long time."

Sammy shook his head. "I don't know if I want to be so mean."

Fern reached out and patted him on his good shoulder. "It's not being mean. He hit you, he hurt you, and he should be prosecuted."

There was a long pause. Sammy wanted to apologize for losing her gift, but he didn't want to bring up the subject.

"Don't worry about anything. Just get better. Joe is keeping your cart safe for you until you get out."

Sammy mumbled, "Good."

A silence seemed to stretch on forever. Then Fern pulled a paper bag out from a pocket in her jacket and handed it to Sammy.

He automatically reached for it. He pulled his hand back, ashamed he hadn't taken better care of the dream-catcher she gave him before.

"Here, take it," she insisted. "After all, it's yours."

A Fleeting Glimpse

Curious, Sammy took the bag and opened it. He saw something blue and sparkly inside.

With a whoop of joy, he pulled out the dream-catcher. It wasn't broken, nor cracked.

"Soon you'll be just as blue again as your dream-catcher," said Fern.

K. E. Swope

The Bare Essentials

Gladys Plumleigh stared in disbelief. From the entrance to the dining room onboard the cruise ship, Harmony Voyager, she saw naked people sitting at the tables. None of them seemed to be under fifty. The only people who wore any clothing were the waiters.

Embarrassed and confused, she turned away abruptly. Her exit was blocked by a deeply tanned man in a white uniform, with too much decoration.

"You are late," he said, shaking a finger at her. His smile and the lilt in his thick Italian accent took away any sting from the action. "You must be Miss Plumleigh, since she is the only name left. Allow me to show you to your table."

Gladys held him back. "I can't go in there," she whispered. "Those people aren't wearing any clothes."

He expanded his smile. "Ah, I understand. There are other shy ones on this first night who prefer to ease into it gradually."

"Ease into what?" Gladys felt a churning in her stomach. What had she gotten into? The travel agent on the telephone had mentioned this new cruise as the only one with openings at such short notice.

Her escort frowned momentarily, then his smile returned. "But of course, you are teasing me, no? We were told to prepare for lots of, how you say, high jinx? Come, your waiter has begun taking orders."

Gladys resisted his efforts to pull her into the room. "I'm not going in there until someone tells me what is going on."

The uniformed man pulled his arm away and drew himself to his full height, smile now gone. "Madame, if you have any problems, I suggest you see the purser."

"Then that's just what I'll do." Gladys consulted the layout of the ship, she found the purser's office on Promenade deck.

"Yes, ma'am? What can I do for you?" asked the blond man behind the counter.

Gladys took a deep breath before starting. She wanted to be kind but firm.

"Well, there seems to be some sort of mistake. Um, the people in the dining room....well, just exactly what kind of cruise is this?"

The man's eyebrows rose until they disappeared under the brim of his cap. "It's a new cruise. The AANR chartered the ship for their annual convention."

"AANR?"

"That's the American Association for Nude Recreation. Surely, you're a member, aren't you?" The man's eyebrows descended to shade his blue eyes. He frowned. "You're not a member, are you? Didn't your travel agent tell you?"

Gladys gasped. She realized she had heard "new" instead of "nude." No wonder Sally at Getaway Tours had asked her repeatedly if she was sure she really wanted to go on this particular cruise.

"There's been some mistake," she finally said. "I've got to get off the ship."

"I'm sorry, but that's impossible once we're at sea. Unless there's a medical emergency. Is that the case?"

Gladys wished she could say there was, because she was sure her blood pressure was skyrocketing. She couldn't, though, because the cruise line would probably bill her for the expense of a helicopter pickup. That was an added expense she couldn't handle on her teacher's salary.

Gladys found a lounge where she could order a sandwich to take to the closet called her cabin, two decks down from the public area. Sitting on the narrow bed, she munched as she fumed. *Misunderstanding, indeed! I can't take off my clothes and parade around in front of a bunch of strangers.*

She glared at her suitcases, still unpacked. Then she noticed papers on the other bed and nearly choked. She had a roommate. *It can't be... they couldn't possibly...no, I will absolutely not share a cabin with a man.*

A Fleeting Glimpse

While she had been checking out the ship's library before dinner, someone else had arrived. Gladys dashed to the closet and threw open the door. Two dresses hung above two pairs of decidedly female shoes.

Relieved, Gladys curled up on her bed to think.

How had she gotten herself in this dilemma? And how was she going to get out of it?

It had been only a few weeks since she overheard a conversation in the teachers' lounge while she was in the adjacent restroom. Her young colleagues had been describing the elaborate New Year's Eve parties they attended.

"Miss Prune was probably curled up with a book instead of a man," whispered Norma Landis too loudly.

"Or watched her laundry go round," Cissy duPont whispered back.

A gale of laughter followed. Gladys knew that her young pupils shortened her name to Miss Plum, but this unseemly joking by her colleagues really hurt. She had taken pains to mentor each new young teacher who joined their faculty so she felt betrayed by their cruel joking.

Did they really see her as a dried-up old woman? In the mirror she saw her face was red, uncertain whether it was from embarrassment or anger. Her face wasn't all that wrinkled for her sixty years. The overhead light did bring out the silver intermingled with her light brown hair. Behind thick eyeglasses, her brown eyes were still bright. Sometimes her hearing played tricks on her and she moved up stairs more slowly than she used to, but otherwise she didn't feel like a dull old woman. Her life revolved around lesson plans, seminars, faculty meetings, and tutoring but nothing else. For her, it was the right life. She hadn't thought about what other people thought of her in many years. *I hope those youngsters look as good after thirty-two years of teaching. After all I've done to mentor them, how can they be so cruel? I'll show them. But what can I do?*

For the rest of the day, Gladys smiled for her students as usual but avoided the other teachers. Luckily no meetings had been scheduled for that afternoon, so she went home after preparing her classroom for the next day.

While lamb chops baked, she finished reading the morning newspaper. She noticed an advertisement: "Charge up your batteries—get away from it all on a cruise." Gladys turned the page and then turned back again. Perhaps that was her answer, to show the other teachers she wasn't the stodgy old woman they considered her. Winter break was coming. Besides, a phone call wasn't a commitment.

"I'm sorry, Miss Plumleigh," said Sally, the woman who answered. "You're much too late to book a cruise for February. Most people reserve their cruises a year in advance to get a better price. Sometimes there's a last-minute cancellation, but there's no guarantee. With only a month before sailing, I doubt I can find a good spot for you. Is that the only week you can go?"

"Yes, it's my winter break. I guess I'll just have to wait. Drat, I was really hoping."

"Don't give up yet," urged Sally. "I can call around to check. Sometimes there are last-minute cancellations. Double occupancy is cheaper than a single, and I may be able to find you a spot as the second occupant."

"You mean, room with a total stranger?"

Sally laughed. "Don't worry. If you run into a real problem, you can always complain to the purser. Cruise ships keep a cabin empty for emergency situations."

"Well, I said I wanted to try something different," admitted Gladys. Somewhere in the middle of the conversation, a cruise became very important to her, something she wanted to do very much—and needed to do soon.

Sally promised to call if she got any fresh information.

At school the next day, Gladys tried to forget the words she had overheard. She thought a few of the new teachers were smirking when she passed them in the hallway. Perhaps she seemed like a dried up old prune to them. She didn't feel that way. She really wanted to do something to prove it.

After school, Gladys hurried home. The blinking light on her answering machine lifted her spirits. Setting down her bag of groceries, Gladys hit the play button.

"Miss Plumleigh, this is Sally at Getaway Tours. It's been tough but I found something for you that week in February, a cancellation." The message paused and picked up some static. "It's definitely different—a week-long new cruise around the Caribbean with stops in Jamaica and Nassau. If you're interested, I need a commitment, including a deposit by tomorrow. I've put a verbal reservation on it, but the cruise line will hold it for only 24 hours."

There it was, a chance to get away. Should she—or shouldn't she?

By the time Gladys decided to call the travel agency, it had closed and she got the answering machine. Hesitantly at first, then becoming more confident, she left a message for Sally to book it.

The next day after school, Gladys dropped off her check at Getaway Tours. Sally apologized because she had no brochures about that particular cruise, but she had several about Voyager itself, including the layout of the ship. She showed Gladys where her cabin would be, just below the water line on the interior of the corridors.

Gladys "accidentally" left one of the brochures on the lunch table in the teachers' lounge. She savored the astonishment of other teachers when she nonchalantly retrieved it later. As she closed the door on her way out, she smiled to herself at the chatter behind her. She knew they were talking about her—and this time she was glad. Watching laundry go around in the dryer, indeed!!

Now she sat in a cabin the size of her bathroom, wishing she were at home, even watching laundry drying.

How could she have not noticed what was going on? Had naked people been walking around her all afternoon, without her noticing? She remembered fully clothed passengers just after arrival, standing with her at the railing as they watched the shoreline recede. She was too excited to partake of the advertised buffet near the pool, especially after the high calorie airline food. While she waited for her luggage to be delivered, she wandered toward the piano player in the cocktail lounge on Lido deck.

There she had discovered the ship had a library. She browsed the titles, mostly mysteries. To her joy, she found one by her favorite author that she hadn't read. She was so immersed in the detective's track of the killer that she barely noticed when the ship pulled away from the pier. She was so intent that she didn't realize how time was passing until her stomach growled. Her wristwatch showed 6:15—and dinner was at six. So she had hurried to dinner and found....

Just then the cabin door opened. In came her cabin mate, a rotund pink figure wearing nothing, unless the green feather boa and pearl necklace could be counted. When she saw Gladys sitting there, fully dressed, a smile lit up her face.

The newcomer said, "Hi, I'm Florence. This your first convention? Most of us are a bit shy the first time."

Gladys nodded, holding her gaze on the woman's face with its double chins. Then she broke down and began to cry.

Florence handed her a box of tissues from the desk. She turned away to retrieve a sheer lilac dressing gown that provided an illusory covering. "Is that better?"

Gladys took off her glasses to wipe her wet cheeks and nodded.

With little coaxing, Florence got the whole story. She had the courtesy not to laugh. "We've got a problem, don't we?"

"We?" Gladys blew her nose and put her glasses back on.

"Of course, WE. How do you expect me to enjoy myself, knowing you're miserable? Besides, I don't know many of the other naturalists. My cousin planned the trip, but had to stay home with her mother who fell and broke her ankle. I was really hoping I'd be lucky enough to get someone nice as a cabin mate to help me break the ice and meet other people. So you see, this affects me, too."

Gladys felt somewhat better. "I can't walk around without clothes on. And how can I possibly avoid staring? Especially at the men." She blushed.

Florence did laugh then. "Lord, there's not much to see. Almost all of us are over the hill." Then she sobered. "I know we say clothing is optional, but you'll be the one stared at if you insist on wearing clothes. Don't you know it's clothing that's provocative, not its absence? It hides and reveals, making suggestions about what's underneath. It's really what stimulates people. Once you reveal all, there's no more secrets and we can be real with each other."

"My head accepts your reasoning, but logic isn't going to help me."

"Well, then, let's try practice. Take off your clothes."

"What!"

A Fleeting Glimpse

"It's just us. No one else will see. We've got to try, or we'll have a long, boring week stuck here in this closet, playing double solitaire."

Gladys reluctantly disrobed, and immediately sat down on her bed again, legs and arms crossed.

Florence deliberately stared at the ceiling. "How's it feel?"

"Strange," admitted Gladys. She uncrossed her arms and stretched. "But sort of nice. Free."

"That's it exactly. Now get up and walk around."

"But I'll jiggle."

Florence chuckled. "Of course, we all do. You can practice walking with more of a slide in your step, rather than a bounce. That helps."

Gladys took a few steps, then tried sliding her feet across the carpeting.

"See?" Florence tossed her lilac wrap on her bed. "Now, look at me."

Gladys did—and turned red all over.

"No, don't look at me. Focus on my eyes or at a spot about a foot above them. That's what all the crew have been told."

Although she followed directions, Gladys found it hard to hold her gaze steady. "I don't think I can do it. My eyes want to look."

She sat down on her bed again. She took off her glasses to wipe the remaining moisture from her cheek. She dropped them when Florence hollered, "That's it."

"What? Where are my glasses?"

"Look at me and tell me what you see."

Gladys squinted. "You look like a pink blob."

Florence grabbed both arms and swung Gladys around the cabin. "There's our answer. Don't wear your glasses."

Gladys stooped down on hands and knees, groping on the floor. "It won't work. How can I find my way around?"

"Easy—we'll just have to stick together."

And that was that. It wasn't easy at first, but Gladys found she could make out shapes enough so that after two days of wandering around the ship, she knew where she was. The only time she wore her glasses was at meals, to read the menu. But that wasn't so bad, since everyone was sitting down.

All too soon the week ended. Gladys and Florence exchanged addresses and phone numbers. Although she hoped they would stay in touch, Gladys resolved not to try any more nude outings.

The first day back at school after winter break was hectic, as usual. In the teachers' lounge, many of the other teachers managed to eat lunch when they knew Gladys had her break. They looked up expectantly, and Norma asked if she enjoyed her cruise.

"Oh, yes, very much."

Cissy remarked, "You certainly have a good tan."

Gladys smiled. "I certainly do."

Norma asked, "Then you'd recommend a cruise as a good get-away?"

"Well, only if you're prepared to make do with the bare essentials."

Going Home

I went home last week.

I was proud of my hand, steady on the doorbell. My stomach wasn't steady, though. It was rumbling and gurgling and roiling, like Old Faithful before it blows.

It took forever for someone to come to the door. I wished I had worn the denim skirt rather than the black suede. I wished I had colored my hair, got rid of the gray. To look more like my younger self, so they'd be sure to recognize me.

Finally I heard footsteps on the hardwood floor of the entry hall. They still hadn't bought carpet, that much hadn't changed. The face at the screen door had.

"Ruthie?" Why did my voice come out as a question? I knew that face, a slightly younger version of my own.

The woman flinched at the name. Then frowned. "Whatever you're selling, we don't want any." She turned, her hand on the inner door to close it.

"Don't you remember me?" My voice was steadier at the second attempt.

The woman peered over her bifocals. "I'm not good at guessing games. I'm busy, so state your business."

I hadn't expected it to be easy. "I'm...I call myself Ebony now. But I was christened Sarah Elizabeth. You were named Mary Ruth two years later." You as Ruthie, me as Lizzy. You, the perfect daughter. Me, the disgrace.

No answering smile. Just a ripple on both cheeks, betraying clenched teeth.

My stomach threatened to turn inside out. No good after all. Too much history. I turned to leave.

"I call myself Mary, no more Ruthie." The woman's voice was barely audible. "Why now?"

I let out my breath. I hadn't realized I was holding it. "Isn't a fiftieth wedding anniversary a good reason? Prodigal son, er, daughter. How about the fatted calf?"

Mary didn't smile. "Still as irreverent and disrespectful as ever."

I felt my face flush. God, with all that's happened, how could I feel embarrassed at this?

I held back the swear words, nearly biting my tongue in the effort. "Please, Ruthie, er, Mary. I've come to wish them well. Even brought a present. Thought I'd smooth out hard feelings, and all that."

Mary's laugh came out as a sharp bark. "Hard feelings? What can you possibly mean? You disappear for, what, twenty, thirty years? Then suddenly, you show up on their doorstep. By the way, you're a day early. The high Mass is being celebrated tomorrow."

I took two deep breaths before answering. "I'm not staying for any church stuff. Just want to wish Mom and Dad…oh, hell, this isn't working." I turned to walk down the steps.

"Wait," Mary called from the doorway. "Don't you think you owe me, us, an explanation? Why did you leave without saying good-bye to me? Where did you go?"

"Didn't they tell you?" Of course they didn't. They hadn't wanted to spoil the perfect daughter. She might get ideas if she knew.

"It's a long story. Look, can I come in? I feel funny standing out here. Does Mrs. O'Malley still keep an eye on everyone who comes by? I'll bet she remembers me."

"Wait, let me prepare them. The shock…."

I nodded. Alone, I did some calculations. Married at age twenty-eight, my mother would be nearly eighty. And my father, he'd be nearly ninety. That damned war.

Mary returned while I was counting. She held open the screen door. "They've changed a lot."

"All of us have."

Inside, I smelled the odors I remembered. Olive oil overheated in the frying pan. Cinnamon. Rose potpourri. A new one, like dirty socks.

"Mom's in the kitchen," said Mary.

"Where else?"

Shared laughter. Mary smiled more sincerely. She touched my wrist lightly. "It's been so long."

"Thirty-five years."

"I missed you so much." Her voice faded.

"It was the right decision...for me."

Mary led the way to the kitchen, as if I didn't know the way. In the doorway, she called out, "Mom, here's Sarah Elizabeth."

A bent-over woman continued rolling out cookie dough without looking up. Sure, swift motions perfected over the years. I inhaled deeply, sugar cookies baking in the oven. How to start?

Mary deftly took the rolling pin from the white-haired woman. "I'll finish while you visit with Sarah Elizabeth."

A frown crossed the wrinkled face. "I was doing just fine." Seeing that resistance was useless, she pulled a cane from beside the table. Without looking at me, she shuffled to a wooden rocking chair next to the stove. Gingerly she lowered herself. "Don't let the ones in the oven burn, Mary!" Then she turned and squinted at me through lenses magnifying her watery brown eyes. "Well, pull over a chair and sit. My neck hurts if I have to look up at you."

I clenched my teeth. Quite a greeting after all this time. I guess I shouldn't have expected anything different. I had to try to connect, for my own peace of mind. Pulling out a chair from the kitchen table, I sat in front of my mother. My skirt hitched up, exposing my knees and part of my thigh.

My mother noticed, of course. She never had approved of what I chose to wear. "Don't you have anything more appropriate for a middle-aged woman?"

Christ on the cross! The woman still knew how to tweak the chain. Why bother trying to make peace? I gritted my teeth to try a new approach, focusing on her. "How have you been, Mom?"

Her liver-spotted hands smoothed the cotton dress hanging well down over her knees.

"Some days better than others. My knee gives me trouble. The doctor wants to replace it, just like the other one. I don't know, though. It took so long to get back on my feet." She went on for several minutes, touching on all her medical problems.

I clenched my teeth. Nothing had changed. No interest in me.

She finally stopped her litany of illnesses and asked, "How are you?"

Surprised, it took me a moment to begin. "Actually, quite well. You see...."

My mother interrupted. "Did I tell you what my cardiologist said last week?"

I glanced over at Mary, who suggested, "Mom, why don't you take her in to Dad. I think he'd like to see her."

"If you say so, dear." She struggled to get up. I tried to help, but my hand was brushed aside. "I'm perfectly capable of taking care of myself."

I stood aside, forcing my hand to my side, preventing it from steadying her wobbly exit.

I followed her out the kitchen door, down the hallway, and into the front room. I had to take tiny steps behind her so that I didn't step on the heels of her threadbare slippers.

My mother entered the sitting room. She took the same seat I remembered so well, a wooden rocking chair surrounded by bags of yarn and knitting needles. Pulling out blue yarn that looked like the back of a child's sweater, she began to rock and knit. Only then did she speak to the person sitting on a recliner. "Hey, Ollie, we got company."

I had waited in the doorway of the familiar room. No changes here. Same upholstery, now a dull brown rather than the chocolate of my childhood. Same photos on the mantle—a wedding portrait from 1945, a girl's high school graduation picture, a mountain scene from a family vacation. Two new ones though, a wedding portrait of Mary Ruth with a man in military uniform and another of two young boys. None of me.

As expected. The man in the recliner hadn't spoken. I walked over to stand in front of him. "Hi, Dad. It's me, Sarah Elizabeth."

His eyes continued to stare at the blank television screen. No expression on his face. The buttons on his shirt had been matched with the wrong buttonholes. Egg stained his trousers. His fly was open. His feet rested on a red plastic hassock, one slipper on and the other on the floor. He said nothing.

I looked at my mother. She continued to rock and knit.

"Doesn't Dad…?"

"Oh, he never says much, a man of few words. Sometimes he sits in that chair for hours without making a sound. He's no trouble to me at all. So don't you start making noises about him going to that home." Her voice rose in volume on the last part.

I turned back to the silent man. "Dad, remember the black kitten you got me when I was little? We called him Two Socks because he had two white paws."

Was that a flicker in his eye? No sound.

"Boy, was I scared when I fell out of the tree. Remember how you told me stitches would make me look like Zorro?"

A twitch of the lips. Still no sound, no eye movement.

I pulled a flat package out of my bag. "I brought a gift for your anniversary. Would you like to see it?"

At that my mother perked up. "Bring it here. I want to open it."

I took it over to my mother. She ripped off the paper. "Oh, it's just a picture." She handed it back.

Christ on a pogo stick, why did I try? I stared at the photograph of me with my daughter, the cause of all the past trouble. No! That wasn't true. Myra had been my blessing, I caused the trouble. I gently placed the framed picture on my father's lap. "This is your granddaughter. I named her Myra after your mother. Grandma was so good to me."

The picture lay on his lap, untouched. I sighed. What a wasted trip. I sensed another person: Mary stood in the doorway.

"Your daughter?"

"Yeah, my daughter, the pediatrician. The Sisters wanted me to give her up, but I couldn't. She was so beautiful, so perfect. So I ran away with her."

Mary's jaw dropped. "You had a baby?"

I laughed. "I'm not surprised they never told you, afraid you'd get ideas too, I guess."

My laughter stopped on a sob. "The Sisters of Mercy took me in, all right. Wanted me to give up my baby for adoption. Then I could go home to my good Catholic family, after a vacation in the mountains, with no one the wiser. Only I wasn't having any of it. The miracle of life.... Anyway, it wasn't easy, but we made it."

Mary put a hand out, then dropped it. I turned to leave. Wasted trip, mother still full of herself and dad even more remote.

Behind me, I heard a sound. I turned. My father's fingers were on the photograph.

"Lizzy?" he whispered hoarsely.

A Fleeting Glimpse

Man to Man

"Do any of us really understand women?" Donald asked his friend Jonathan on that last camping trip. The words lingered in Jonathan's memory. He and Don had shared so many things over the years, even women. But no longer.

Before they met on friendly terms, they had faced each other as competitors on football fields and basketball courts in high school. It was orange and blue versus blue and white. Kill the Trojans! Slaughter the Rams! Win! Score! Just don't become friends.

In the late fifties, Jonathan's family was considered rich. The Long family store flourished, while his mother cared for the family and the house. Jonathan attended the town's only public high school. His grades were typical of the times—good enough to get into college but not so good that they hampered his social acceptance. Life was perfect, in Jonathan's view, until his father's good deed complicated it.

The private high school across town was the public school's arch rival in everything from scholastic awards to sports championships. Called an "industrial" school, it educated orphans from all over the state, boys who lived in groups on farms in the surrounding countryside, thanks to the generosity of a wealthy philanthropist. The "farm boys" were looked down on because they were different—they didn't have "normal" families and they were born elsewhere. They just didn't belong. But they sure could play football and basketball, Jonathan remembered.

Jonathan first met Donald off the playing fields the summer before their junior year in high school. When a local civic organization decided to provide a semblance of normal living for the farm boys, Jonathan's father volunteered. It meant inviting one boy to the Long home once a month.

"But, Dad, you can't!" Jonathan protested. "They're the enemy. What will Coach Jasper say? And the other guys on the team? They won't trust me anymore."

His father ignored his very good reasons, determined to set a good example for the community. Jonathan's two sisters sided with their father because they hoped "their" boy would be cute. His mother just said, "Be nice, Jon."

On that first "Adopt an Orphan" day, the whole town turned out on the town green to participate directly or just observe. Among screaming children, barking dogs, and boring speakers, Jonathan sat with his family on a stiff folding chair and stared at his shoes, too glum to even look at the boys. Finally the last speaker sat down and the school band played a fan fare. Time for the selection.

"Psst, look, Jon," said his younger sister, poking him in the ribs. "Which one do you think is ours? I hope it's not the one with that hideous red hair."

Jonathan looked up at the boys on the sun-baked platform. Two rows of identical navy blue suits sat numbly behind the podium. Most of them held heads down and stared at the wooden planking as if reading their fate among the splinters. The announcer began to call names.

"Anderson family. Adams, Sinclair."

A red-faced boy stood up at the end of the first row, took one hesitant step toward the speaker, and stopped in confusion when no one from the audience stood up.

The announcer repeated the call. "Anderson family. Are they here?"

A stooped woman in the last row of chairs on the green stood up and raised a hand. "Aye, we're here. Can you send him on back? It's hard on me back to walk so far."

Sinclair Adams walked unsmiling down the aisle toward his benefactors, head high and eyes straight ahead. Jonathan turned and watched him go by.

After that, the match-ups went smoothly.

"Beam family. Cantor, Irwin."

"Becker family. Davis, Marvin."

And so on down the list. Jonathan watched the boys remaining on stage, on display like prize cattle going to the highest bidder. He almost felt sorry for them, but not quite. He couldn't forget the teasing and suspicions that had faced him at football practice the previous day.

"Long family. Hardy, Donald."

"He's short," whispered Jonathan's older sister.

"He's got freckles," said the younger.

As his family walked forward between the rows of fellow townspeople, Jonathan looked up from beneath lowered eyelids. There stood the enemy, a brown-haired, ordinary looking boy with a square body and freckles. Was that Hardy the Hare? How could that body move fast enough to gain the reputation as the fastest quarterback in the state? Was that "Hare-brain" Hardy, a whiz at set plays on the basketball court? Somehow the enemy looked less intimidating, even tame, in this uniform of navy blue.

Jonathan remembered to force a smile when his sisters poked him in the ribs from opposite sides. He realized that the others had been introducing themselves. Awkwardly he stuck out his right hand to shake and looked into the darkest pair of eyes he'd ever seen.

"Hi," said freckle-faced Hare-brain, with a slight quaver.

"Hi," mumbled Jonathan. Could the famous Hardy the Hare be nervous?

The day went downhill from there. Mrs. Long played mother hen, Mr. Long grilled Donald about his life's history, and Jonathan's sisters giggled every time their guest answered his inquisitor. As for Jonathan, he shoveled in the food and tried to ignore the interchanges. At the end of the meal, he could no longer distance himself from his unwelcome guest. Mrs. Long called her daughters into the kitchen to help wash dishes and Mr. Long retreated to the living room to read the Sunday paper between long blinks. That left the two rivals to face each other.

Donald began, "I'm sorry...."

At the same time, Jonathan said, "By the way...."

Both stopped in confusion. Donald's face turned so red that his freckles were camouflaged. Then they looked directly at each other and burst out laughing.

Years later, when the two compared notes about that day, Jonathan found out that Donald had been even more embarrassed and reluctant to participate than had Jonathan. However, as a scholar athlete, Donald had no choice but to follow the orders of his coach and principal if he wanted to be considered for college scholarships. Trying to project the proper image to the townspeople, they had told him, meant they needed him and the others to show what type of boys were attending the industrial school. It was called public relations.

During those last two years of high school, Donald continued his monthly visits to the Long family as "their" orphan. His conversations with Jonathan loosened up somewhat, although they never became free and easy—any talk about sports brought on extended pauses while each decided how much to say without giving away team strategies.

It was in college that their friendship really developed. After being intense rivals, they suddenly found themselves on the same team. Jonathan followed the family tradition of attending Penn State, with Donald obtaining a full scholarship to the same school. Although they were given different roommates at the start of freshman year, they learned to know each other during the long drives back and forth between college and Jonathan's home. Somehow those monthly visits during high school had become such a habit it was understood that, naturally, Donald would come along "home" with Jonathan.

Both of them were popular with classmates and had no lack of dates. Somehow Jonathan found himself deeply involved with a girl he had known in high school, although that didn't stop him from playing the field when he stayed on campus. Despite his popularity, Donald kept his dates at arm's length, enjoying each girl's company for a time, but eventually moving on to the next one.

Finally, graduation came—time to face the real world. And time to go their separate ways. Just a month before the big day, Jonathan suddenly realized their idyllic existence was coming to an end. He was headed for the family business, no question about that, and would probably marry his long-time girlfriend. He also realized he had no idea what Donald planned to do. The subject had never come up. Jonathan finally just blurted out the question.

"So, Don, what will you do now?"

They were using a quiet moment to go through their collected papers and books, trying to decide what to trash and what was worth keeping. Jonathan noticed that Donald's pile to throw out was much larger than his keeper stack.

Donald looked up with an impish grin. "Thought I'd be a bum for a while."

Jonathan laughed. "Right. Don't you think we've done enough of that lately? That redhead sure won't forget you for a long time!"

"Yeah." The grin disappeared. "Seriously, I'm going to head west for a bit, see what I can find."

"But...but...aren't you going to get a job?"

Donald shrugged. "Sure, eventually. Right now, though, I need to resolve some things before I get on with my life."

"Things? What things?"

A sigh. "I need to see where my dad died. They never recovered his body, so we never had a proper funeral. The uncertainty was what killed my mom finally."

"I'm sorry...I didn't know...you never...." Jonathan faltered, not knowing what to say.

Donald looked up with his usual grin. "It's okay. Just something I have to do." He hesitated. "That's why I can't seem to get serious about any one girl. Part of me wants to get married and have lots of kids, but part of me holds back because I'm afraid of hurting someone by loving too much."

Jonathan busied himself with leafing through the book in his hands, not really seeing the contents. He couldn't think of anything to say.

Donald sighed. "But after that, I plan on heading right back to you and see about getting a job. After all, you're about the only family I've got."

It took over a year, but Donald did return, as promised. One day he walked into Long's hardware as if he were a regular customer. The next day he started work as Jonathan's marketing manager. Jonathan's wife, Marge, liked him, too. As soon as she discovered he was unmarried, she set her mind to changing that, with her specific candidate being her friend, Phoebe. Within five years of his return, Donald married Phoebe, giving in to her sweet nature and to Marge's persuasive power.

The only conversation about those missing months, held just before the wedding, was brief.

Jonathan asked, over an inventory sheet, "By the way, when you went west, did you find what you were looking for?"

Donald kept his eyes on his own list. "Yep."

"Want to talk about it?"

"Nope."

"You okay?"

"Yep."

That was the extent of Jonathan's probe into his friend's search. The two friends became a foursome, and the hardware store prospered under their complementary skills. But they became just a twosome once a year, in the spring, for a week of camping and fishing.

Jonathan could still close his eyes and see the layout of their last campsite, gear neatly stowed and cooler of beer sitting just out of reach of the fire's heat but close enough to pull out another bottle without getting up. A campsite like all the previous ones, except this time Donald got stinking drunk.

Both of them had held their liquor well in college. If they were paired in a keg race, they nearly always drank the whole thing before any other team could get started properly…and still walk in a circle without falling down. Over the years, they continued to enjoy a cold lager together, but became moderate drinkers.

On that last trip, Donald started it after his tenth bottle. "So, do you understand women?"

"Of course not. We're not supposed to. Have another." Jonathan pulled out two more bottles.

"Thanks." Donald took a long swig. "I don't understand why women can never be satisfied with what they've got."

"What's up? Phoebe want a new car?"

Donald took another long swallow. "Nah, not Phoebe." He hiccuped. "Marge."

"Yeah, Marge always wants something and she usually gets what she wants."

Donald burst out laughing, then choked. Jonathan thumped him on the back until he got his breath back.

"You okay?"

Nodding, Donald took another swallow, a small one this time to ease his burning throat.

"Yeah, hunky dory." He looked up at his friend with bleary eyes, then down at the ground.

"You've always been a good friend, and...."

"Aw, shucks, twarn't nothin'."

"No, I mean it. You and your folks made me feel like I belonged. That meant a lot. My dad...." He stopped and shook his head. "No, I won't be like him. Jon, I've got to tell you. I feel like such a louse...."

"You're a louse awright. It's 'cause of you that my business can compete with the chain across town. Here's to you, louse." Jonathan raised his bottle and waved it around before taking another gulp.

"Will you listen to me?" Donald spoke so quietly that Jonathan put down his bottle to listen. "I'm tired of hiding it, your wife has been chasing me ever since I got back to town. And you know she doesn't give up when she wants something."

Jonathan sat stunned. He raised his beer as if to take a drink, looked at it in confusion, and heaved it into the bushes. "God."

Silence. The darkness surrounding them was also silent, no night noises. Only the crackle of the flames.

"I don't know...didn't know...." Jonathan began but stopped in confusion. Finally he stammered out, "And?"

"And what? You want me to tell you how many time I've slept with your wife. You want me to tell you what I did to her? How I pleasured her? How I....?

Jonathan's fist hit Donald's face before he could get out the next words.

Donald raised a hand to his mouth to wipe away a trickle of blood. "I'm sorry." He looked at the red mark on his hand. "I'm bloody well sorry." He got up and stumbled into the bushes.

Jonathan sat, staring at the flames consuming the birch log. He saw faces—his father, his mother, his sisters, but, most of all, Don's. In that ridiculous navy blue suit the first time they met, in his football jersey, his basketball shirt. In his wedding tuxedo. Then he saw Marge's face, her piercing eyes and set mouth, reflecting her will to get whatever she wanted.

Finally, he shook his head and looked over to his friend, to apologize or to continue the fight, he wasn't sure. But Donald wasn't there. He sure was taking a long time to relieve himself. Maybe he needed time to think, too.

Jonathan lurched to his feet and stumbled toward a nearby bush to return his own beer to the earth. He tripped over a root, then crawled into his sleeping bag. Too much beer and too much talk. Tomorrow, they'd sort it out.

The funeral was three days later. The coroner's assessment was death from a blow to the head sustained when Donald fell down a ravine in the dark. No one questioned Jonathan too closely, but expressed sympathy at his loss of such a good friend and employee. Only Marge looked at him with questions in those eyes.

Breakdown

Rosa was on her way home, the sun in her eyes on this late November day. She would have been there by now if she hadn't picked up her office phone. Somehow, she had become the person the switchboard usually chose to receive calls from disgruntled customers.

Suddenly there was an ominous rattle from under her car. Then the noise stopped.

Oh, no, did she run over something. The noise didn't feel or sound like a flat tire.

The next few miles passed quietly, as the sun slipped behind the trees lining the road. This was the loneliest stretch of road on her way home with no houses along the road.

Then the rattle came back. It soon became a clanking. Once more the noise stopped.

She thought about pulling over, just to look under the car. Even with a flashlight, she wouldn't know what she was looking at if she did see something different. Little traffic came this way, so by stopping she'd just be making her trip take more time. She decided to just keep going, only about another four miles to her home.

Then, for the third time, more noise came back. This time there was no pause, just continuous sounds of metal scraping along the pavement. The only thing that kept her calm was a lack of warning lights on her dashboard displays.

A few cars passed her, going in the opposite direction. Some drivers turned their heads to stare at the racket her car was making, but they all kept going. Rosa felt that someone would flag her down if flames were pouring out from under her car.

The uninterrupted clattering started to make her nervous. It was worse than fingernails screeching along a chalkboard. Perhaps she had run over something and was dragging it with her. Perhaps she could dislodge it. Just ahead was a small parking lot for a nail salon that had gone out of business. She could pull safely off the road. She slowed and turned in. At least her car still went where she steered it, so whatever had happened couldn't be too bad.

Grabbing her flashlight, she got out of the car and knelt down to look underneath.

The flashlight didn't show any light. That's what happened when she didn't check the batteries often enough. As cars passed by, they shed enough light for her to see a piece of metal hanging down under there. It was about the size of a loaf of bread, and it was still attached to the car. Not the muffler, it was too far forward. Whatever it was, it couldn't be too important because her engine had still been working fine. She feared, though, that continuous dragging would pull off something more vital to her car's operation.

With a sigh, she stood up and pulled out her cell phone. She would call for a tow, just to be safe. She didn't need to pay for major auto repairs on top of her other bills.

No luck, the phone was dead. She had meant to recharge it last night but forgot.

Looking around in the dark, she saw no nearby occupied buildings.

She thought about flagging down a passing motorist, but hesitated. It could be dangerous to stop a stranger along such a deserted roadway.

Just then, a car pulled off the road to park behind her. The headlights stayed on so she couldn't see the driver.

Rosa quickly jumped into her car and locked the doors. Why was the other driver just sitting there? She fastened her seat belt, prepared to drive away if she felt threatened, noise or no noise. Then the headlights behind her suddenly switched off and the car door opened. The inside light showed the head of a man as he stepped out. Rosa sat with the key in the ignition and her hand ready to start up the instant she felt threatened.

A Fleeting Glimpse

In her rearview mirror she could see the outline of a tall, rangy man as passing headlights played over him. He wore an open jacket and his arms swung loosely at his sides. He didn't seem too threatening, but Rosa kept her hand on the key in the ignition.

The thud of work boots stopped beside her driver's door and the man leaned over. His raggedly cut hair hung nearly in his eyes; his chin sprouted at least a day's growth of graying whiskers. At least his mouth was smiling. He made a motion for her to open the side window.

Rosa complied but she let it down only an inch. Far enough for sound to pass through but not a hand to grab her.

"Need some help?"

His voice was a low baritone and had a hint of authority somehow.

"I think so."

"What seems to be the trouble?"

"My car started making these horrible clanking sounds. I pulled off because I was afraid of damaging the engine. I'm waiting for someone to come."

"Oh, if someone's coming."

With that he turned and began to walk away.

Rosa realized that he was the only one who had paid any attention to her predicament, even though lots of cars had passed by. She had heard too many stories of strangers preying on women traveling alone. The problem she had was that it was getting late, and she was worried no one else would bother to stop. Besides, he had a kind smile and a beautiful voice, despite needing a shave.

"Wait, please. I'm not sure if anyone will come. But how can I know to trust you?"

The man turned slowly. A broad grin creased his face.

"Good reaction. It so happens I'm with the Grayson police department."

"Don't you have a uniform and badge?"

"I'm off duty."

"You must have some identification."

The man pulled out his wallet and held up a driver's license against her window.

"Thank you, Jason Hewitt, for coming to my rescue."

For a moment, a look of confusion passed over the man's face. Then he saluted her casually with two fingers.

"Just a white knight, ma'am."

What was that temporary hesitation? Had he stolen the ID? And why didn't it identify him as a policeman. But she quickly realized she had few options. Anyone else who might stop could be more dangerous. This man with such a devastating smile couldn't be bad, could he? And she didn't really want to be left sitting in her car all night.

"Okay, you could call a tow truck for me."

He flashed another gorgeous smile. "You could be waiting here a long time. How about I give you a lift to Mike's garage. It's just down the road. With any luck, he'll still be there."

Rosa hesitated. Hoping she wouldn't regret her decision, she unfastened her seat belt and caught up her purse. She drew a deep breath before unlocking the door. Jason stepped back just enough for her to open the door and climb out. When he held out he hand, she flinched and sat back as far as she could in her seat.

"Is something wrong" he asked with a frown wrinkling his forehead. "I was just going to help you out."

"Oh," replied Rosa, feeling a bit foolish. "I'm not used to such helpful gestures from the men I know."

"Maybe you need to get to know a better class of men."

Rosa found herself chuckling. He seemed to have a sense of humor, so he probably was a nice guy.

As they walked side by side to his car, Jason was careful not to crowd her. He gave her enough personal space that she began to relax a bit.

"So you know my name. What's yours?"

"Rosa Grant." That came out before she thought about it. Was it such a good idea to give this stranger her real name? Perhaps she should have made up a false one. His light-hearted jest had put her at ease. Maybe that wasn't such a good thing.

When in his car, she noticed that the upholstery was ripped and the interior smelled of cigarettes and other odors that she didn't want to identify. Did policemen drive around in such beat-up junk, even their personal ones? She felt the tension build up again.

When he got in, he started up and began pulling out into traffic.

Rosa asked, "Aren't you going to fasten your seat belt?"

"Habit. Sometimes I have to react to emergency calls that I can't lose precious seconds unhooking it."

It sounded plausible, but Rosa still felt unsure of his intentions. Maybe she should unhook hers too so she could react more quickly to any threats. Somehow habit wouldn't let her forgo that safety net in case of an accident.

The sun had completely disappeared by now and the sky was as dark as the building they were approaching. The only light was from a sign that proclaimed "Mike's Lube and Oil."

"I guess he had a slow day and closed early," admitted Jason.

"Yeah," Rosa admitted. To herself, she added, but why wouldn't a police officer know that? Besides no signs said anything about towing and having a mechanic on the premises. She added, "My roommate will be worried if I don't get home soon."

"I'll tell you what," suggested Jason." How about I drive you home and you can decide what to do later?"

Although the suggestion seemed logical, Rosa felt reluctant to have a stranger know where she lived. And to know that there was no roommate waiting for her. Even if he was a police officer.

She had an idea. "Isn't Corinne's Diner just up the road?'

Her chauffeur glanced over to her.

She continued, "I was working so late I didn't have time to eat, so I'd really like to grab a bite to eat before I go home."

Jason turned his eyes back to the road, but not before Rosa saw a quick smile. She hadn't fooled him one bit. "How will you get home?"

"Oh, I can call a cab from there."

She hadn't decided whether Jason was a good guy or not. He had slowed for a stoplight, so Rosa gripped the door handle, ready to throw open the door and jump out. People in the diner would notice if he tried anything. She could scream for help.

Her escape plan wasn't necessary, for the car eased its way into the diner's parking lot and stopped.

"Look," said Jason, "I'd like to stay and make sure you…"

"I've taken up too much of your time."

She quickly opened her door and jumped out of his battered car. In the bright lights of the diner she could see the rust marks and dents in the older model sedan.

"Thank you for stopping."

Then she ran up the steps into the diner before he could follow. When she got safely inside, she turned around to see him still sitting there, watching her.

Rosa sat at the counter and ordered a diet soda and a bowl of chicken soup. While she waited for her order, she looked around for a pay phone. She didn't see one.

She asked the waitress, "Do you have a phone I could use?"

The woman shook her head. "Took out the pay phone cuz everyone's got cells. Got a problem?"

"My car broke down and my cell phone is dead. I was hoping to call a cab from here."

"No problem, I've got Tony's Blue Cab on speed dial."

At Rosa's look, the woman chuckled. "You'd be surprised how many drunks come in for coffee to sober up and then realize it didn't work. The smart ones do, that is."

Before long a brilliant blue minivan pulled up outside. Bright orange letters on the side displayed "Tony's Blue Rides." Rosa saw no sign of Jason's battered sedan in the lot.

Back in her apartment, Rosa double locked her door. She took her first real deep breath of the evening.

After a quick shower, she sat down to check her messages. Before long the phone rang. There was no caller ID, but sometimes people's cell phones didn't register the names or numbers. Rosa picked up the receiver, suspecting one of her coworkers had an emergency. They always seemed to call her when they needed help.

"Hello?"

"Rosa?" It was a man's voice, not one she recognized.

"Yes. Who is this?"

"It's, er, Jason Hewitt. I wanted to make sure you got home safely."

"How did you get my number?"

"You do have a listed number."

Rosa suddenly felt a chill.

"Yes, I did. It was nice of you to check. Thanks again for rescuing me."

A Fleeting Glimpse

She quickly hung up. The idea of a phone listing gave her an idea. She checked local towns for "Jason Hewitt." No such entry. Perhaps he had an unpublishes number.

Who was Jason Hewitt? Was he really a policeman? Was he indeed a good Samaritan who had stopped to help her? That issue she'd deal with tomorrow, right after she called for her car to be towed. She finally felt relaxed enough to sleep after three glasses of her favorite Merlot. The last image she saw before drifting off was a smiling face with graying whiskers.

When her alarm blared in the morning, Rosa groaned. Her mouth felt fuzzy and her shoulder muscles were sore, probably from the tension of the night before. After two cups of coffee, Rosa felt ready to face the day.

First task was to take care of her car. She called the garage down the street from her apartment, knowing that their mechanic got in early. Jimmy hadn't let her down yet in taking care of her late model sedan. She gave him directions to where she left it and promised to send a courier to him with the car keys when she got to work.

Once there, her boss called her in before Rosa could begin to access her messages. Mrs. Anderson wanted her at a lunch-time meeting to prepare for a rush job. The vice president needed a team to bid on a government contract that could mean several million dollars for the company if they won the contract. She wanted Rosa to be in charge of preparing the document.

"Give me a list of writers and typists you want to work on this project. You know the ones who are precise in their work because the deadline is two weeks. I need that list by ten o'clock so I can clear them from other projects.

Rosa groaned inwardly. Sometimes she wished she could afford to mess up so she didn't get put on the hot seat for all the quick turn-around jobs that the brass thought were most important to the welfare of the company.

By ten o'clock Rosa finished her list of the most dependable workers and delivered it to Mrs. Anderson. Then she could check her own waiting in-box and get to her own list of tasks.

It was quick work to get a courier to take her car keys to the garage, but then she faced a more difficult call.

At the local police department, her call was answered within a minute.

"Grayson Police, how may I direct your call?"

"Um, I'd like to speak with one of your officers, Jason Hewitt."

"One moment. I'll connect you with someone who can help you."

Rosa waited and waited. What could be taking so long? Either he was there or he wasn't. Or he wasn't a police officer at all. She had suspected that was the case, especially driving that beat-up old car. If he had misrepresented himself, what could be the reason? He hadn't hurt her or even made any threats. His actions seemed to be meant well, but what was his motive. As a policeman he would feel it part of his duty to help her, but otherwise, what could she think?

Finally a new voice came on the line. "I'm sorry but we don't have an officer with that name on our roster. May I ask who you are and why you're inquiring?"

"Never mind."

Rosa quickly hung up. The receiver clattered as she replaced it because her hands were shaking. The ring of her phone startled her.

"Hello?"

"It's time for the meeting," said the voice of her supervisor.

Rosa forced herself to pay attention to the discussion around her. Somehow, she made notes on what the vice president expected, but she let Mrs. Anderson handle questions for the document production department.

Shortly after lunch, Jimmy called. "Good news. It was only the cover for the catalytic converter that came loose and was dragging."

"What do you need to do?"

"Well, you could replace it, but it means replacing the whole assembly. I can't get just the cover because all this stuff is modular now."

"Ouch, that sounds expensive."

"Or I could just take the cover off completely."

"Will the car be safe to drive without it?"

Jimmy's chuckle came through clearly. "Sure, just don't park on any dry grass. A hot catalytic converter can start a fire and the whole car could burn up. The cover prevents that."

A Fleeting Glimpse

Rose agreed to removing the cover. She knew it would be safe because all the parking lots she used were paved. Jimmy promised to park the car near her apartment. Rosa sighed with relief now that her little adventure had ended happily enough. Except for the mysterious stranger.

Leaving work at her usual time, Rosa headed for the bus stop on the next block. She noticed a dark sedan parked across from her company. As she boarded the bus, she saw that car pull out, make a U-turn, and follow. When she got off at the stop near her apartment, the car kept going.

"Am I getting paranoid?"

The only answer was a soft "meow" from a passing cat. Was that yes or no?

She found her car parked half a block away with a note from Jimmy inside. Probably the bill. She could worry about that in the morning.

When Rosa pulled the curtains before turning on her living room lights, she noticed a dark sedan parked across the street from her building. Was it the same car?

After checking that the chain and bolt on her apartment door were securely fastened, she tried to read the newspaper. Her thought kept straying to the scruffy face of Jason Hewitt.

In her dreams she was being chased by cars full of men with facial hair. Every time she escaped them, she found herself confronting a man with dark eyes nearly hidden by his hair.

In the morning, the first thing she did, even before starting the coffee pot, was to open the curtains and check the parked cars on her street. No sign of the dark car, just a man sitting at the bus stop reading a newspaper. Just then the bus pulled up, but when it left, that man was still sitting there. Was she being stalked?

When she reached her desk, she found her inbox full of urgent demands from different writers in the software department. She spent the morning monitoring two user manuals that need to be delivered later that week.

At lunch time, Rosa decided to walk across the street to a favorite deli rather than ordering a delivery. She needed fresh air and took a deep breath. Someone, somewhere was burning leaves, against city ordinance but that didn't stop the practice. The pungent odor reminded her of her childhood, when it was safe to walk the streets and stalkers were unknown.

Catching sight of a dark sedan parked down the block made her nearly choke on her deep breath. Shaking off her suspicions, Rosa crossed the street and ordered her salad. Instead of eating inside the deli, she decided to eat at her desk so she could make more progress on the pile of documents awaiting her attention.

She finished what needed her immediate attention in time to catch an early bus home. When she got off the bus, she noticed a dark sedan parked across the street from her apartment. She decided to call the police to notify them of the strange car that seemed to be following her. Just in case something happened.

This call was easier for her. The bored voice at the other end asked for particulars about the car and a description of the driver. After being reassured that patrols in her neighborhood would be alert for strangers, Rosa hung up. She felt less than satisfied, but there was nothing else she could do. Unless she were actually attacked, the police probably wouldn't take her concerns seriously.

She tossed and turned at night for the next week. At work, she tried to focus on her tasks and managed to finished the immediate demands. Deep down, though, she knew that her results were less precise than usual and hoped no one would notice.

On Friday afternoon, she decided to drive upstate to visit her sister for the weekend, just to get out of town. Grabbing a can of pepper spray, she checked out the spy hole before opening her door. A man stood outside. With close-cropped hair and a badge, he looked like a policeman. Leaving the chain attached, she opened the door.

"Miss Grant?" His baritone seemed vaguely familiar.

"Yes?"

"I'm with the Grayson police department. I understand you've been concerned about a possible stalker."

Finally someone seemed to be paying attention to her fears. Rosa was still cautious.

"Can I see some identification, please?"

A Fleeting Glimpse

The man placed his photo badge and policeman's shield in front of the spy hole. The badge identified him as Lance Johnson, and the picture matched the man outside her door.

Relieved, Rosa unhooked the chain and opened the door fully.

"I don't mean to be rude, but some strange things have been happening to me lately. Please come in."

She set the can of pepper spray on an end table. Officer Johnson nodded at the movement with a quick smile passing across his lips.

"I see you're being careful, ma'am."

Rosa let out a sound between a laugh and a sob. "If I were really careful I would have kept my cell phone charged and made sure my flashlight batteries worked."

The officer stood just inside the door, passing his hat from hand to hand. "I can appreciate that." He cleared his throat but didn't seem to find his next words.

Suddenly feeling more in charge of the situation, Rosa decided to be gracious. "Please sit down. Can I get you something to drink? Soda? Coffee?"

"No, thanks," he replied, sitting down on the offered upholstered chair.

Again he cleared his throat. What was wrong with the man?

Finally, he sighed. "I understand you were inquiring about one of our officers, a Jason Hewitt."

"Yes," said Rosa, but then shook her head. "But I was told there was no such person affiliated with the Grayson police department. And I didn't leave my name, so how did you find me?"

"Well, ma'am, I owe you an explanation. You see, I was Jason Hewitt."

Rosa felt her jaw drop open. Then she had to laugh.

"I don't think so."

Office Johnson grinned, a gorgeous smile she remembered from the night of her breakdown.

"Really, I am," he said, shrugging his shoulders.

Rosa shook her head. "You don't look the same, and he didn't have a uniform."

"I was undercover, infiltrating a gang smuggling untaxed cigarettes across the border from Canada and distributing them throughout the

Northeast. Our fair city seems to be the center of their operation. I couldn't come out of my deception till that case wound up."

"But you looked so different."

"Scruffy, I know. Had I kept my hair short and my clothing neat, my appearance would have shouted 'cop' to all the crooks involved."

Rosa nodded. "I see. But, has someone really been following me?"

"I asked the guys to keep an eye on you in case any of my targets saw us together and decided to confront you."

"Oh, I guess that makes sense."

"Besides," he admitted sheepishly, "I decided I wanted to see you again, as my real self."

A Fleeting Glimpse

K. E. Swope

ACKNOWLEDGMENTS

Thanks to the faculty in the graduate program at Wesleyan University for helping a math and science person to appreciate the intricacies of literature. In obtaining a Master of Arts in Liberal Studies, I ventured to generate fiction of my own.

Thanks to the Mystic River Writers' Group, who welcomed a novice into their ranks. Their critiques helped me to improve my early efforts. Later I was aided by many in other writing groups at the Groton Library, Waterford Library, and Borders.

Many thanks to Gwen Mariani, who has been instrumental in encouraging me to get my writing published. Without her to "push," my stories would probably still be on a big pile in my closet.

Most of all, my grateful thanks to Robin Nelson at Leaning Rock Press for shepherding me through the process of publication.

Without these people who have touched my life, this volume would not have come into being.

Thank you all.

About the Author

K. E. Swope was born in south central Pennsylvania in 1943. She became a teacher, but inside she remembered the road past her parent's home and how she wished she could see what was at the other end. After teaching, she took time off for two growing boys and later became a technical writer. With her husband's encouragement, she did follow some new roads—among others, she became a licensed soccer referee, drove a race car and climbed the Great Wall of China. Now retired, she lives in southeastern Connecticut.

K. E. Swope with her husband

Milton Keynes UK
Ingram Content Group UK Ltd.
UKHW011422130624
444110UK00019B/463